ISSASARA'S WILL

Jacques Lafarge

Works by Jacques Lafarge

Plays

Planet for sale*
Positive discrimination
The coach despite himself
Psychanalyric*

Short stories

Camille and the baby stork*
Who is I, who is me*?
Back to the convent*
The mechanic and the beautiful car

Novel

The true story of Lazare Meradec

* text in english available on
www.jacqueslafarge.fr

Jacques Lafarge

ISSASARA'S WILL

Novel

Copyright © 2025 Jacques Lafarge

Édition : BoD - Books on Demand, 31 avenue Saint-Rémy,
57600 Forbach, bod@bod.fr
Impression : Libri Plureos GmbH, Friedensallee 273,
22763 Hamburg (Allemagne)
ISBN : 978-2-8106-2947-3
Dépôt légal : Février 2025

CONTENT

PREFACE..9
PROLOGUE...11
THEODOSSIS...21
THE EXPLOSION...47
KEPHTI..65
ISSESSINAK..91
THE DAWO DISTRICT...119
FURUMARK..145
THE HUNT..173
ISSASARA...195
EPILOGUE..213

PREFACE

The Minoan civilisation developed on Santorini and Crete for over a thousand years, until around 1450 BC. Little is known of its origins and history, partly because its writing has never been deciphered. In 1967, archaeologist Spyridon Marinatos discovered a city on Santorini buried under tens of meters of ash deposited by the eruption that ravaged the island in 1628 BC. Excavations revealed a flourishing civilisation that traded with the entire Mediterranean, particularly Egypt, Cyprus, present-day Turkey and Greece. The buildings and streets are in a remarkable state of preservation but, unlike Pompeii, no human remains have been found. Clearly, sensing the danger, the inhabitants had time to flee their city. The eruption made Santorini uninhabitable for several centuries. In Crete, it had little-known consequences, but it appears that, at the beginning of the 15th century BC, the island had become Mycenaean.

In this novel, I imagine what, after the eruption of Santorini, could have led to a thousand-year-old civilisation being supplanted by another in a few decades. To write it, I based myself on archaeological data. The places correspond to the Minoan cities whose remains can be visited today, and the elements of daily life correspond to what can be deduced from the structures and objects found. On the other hand, the story is a fiction whose events and characters are imaginary. Only the beginning (the eruption of Santorini) and the end (the Mycenaean colonisation) are historical facts.

Jacques Lafarge

PROLOGUE

The finger hovering above the mouse button, Aristotle Kondopoulos hesitates one last time before clicking on "Send" with a small smile of satisfaction. He knows his message will spread far beyond the microcosm of specialists in Minoan civilisation, reaching archaeologists, historians, sociologists, and linguists worldwide. It must be said that he managed his effects well. He simply wrote: *"I am pleased to inform you that following an exceptional discovery at the site of Aghia Triada, we have been able to unveil most of the great mysteries of Minoan civilisation. You will soon be informed of the date and location of a conference we will hold on this subject."*

Six months later, he insisted that the presentation take place in Santorini, at the Petros Nomikos conference centre, even though it was far too small to accommodate all the scientists who would not want to miss the event. He assured everyone that his choice would make sense during his presentation.

The excitement of major scientific events reigns in the packed conference room. Despite technical difficulties and logistical challenges at the entrance, the event is already two hours behind schedule. Many are standing or even sitting on the floor, but no one complains, thrilled to witness the event live. To handle the overflow, video broadcasts have been set up in every annex of the conference centre, with additional streams organised hastily in hotels on the island equipped with projection facilities.

Finally, the main hall doors close. Aristotle takes the podium. Silence descends. While the lights dim, the first slide appears behind him. As the image becomes legible, murmurs ripple through the room. When everyone can clearly read "WELCOME TO HATTIARINA," the hubbub is at its peak. Jubilating, Aristotle starts with the immutable phrases of welcome and thanks to which speakers oblige themselves before their presentation. Usually, no one listens to these foreplays. That day, you can't even hear them. Aristotle has all the difficulty in the world to calm his audience.

"Well! I think it's time to end the suspense before we have a riot. Welcome to Hattiarina! This message alone summarises the extraordinary results we have achieved. Ladies and gentlemen, we now know the name the people we call Minoans used for themselves, we know the names of their islands and cities, we know their language, and we even know where they came from."

It looks like a freeze frame. Excitement has given way to stupefaction.

"You may wonder how such a result is possible from a single discovery. Well, here it is: three years ago, I was working on the site of Aghia Triada. While trying to clear an oil press, I discovered a pot hidden in the wall of the workshop where I was digging. It was filled with wood ash in which six documents were perfectly preserved: two papyri and four clay tablets."

"The papyri have been dated to between 1550 and 1600 BCE. The tablets are disks, similar to the Phaistos Disk but slightly larger, with text written in a spiral on both sides. Together, they constitute what we have all dreamed of: the same text written using two scripts, one known and one unknown. Specifically, two discs are written in the Minoan language using Linear A script. and the other two in archaic Greek using Linear B script ."

The audience immediately understands that Aristotle has succeeded in deciphering Linear A, the famous Minoan script that has long resisted the best experts. Conversations break out across the room.

"I see that I do not need to explain to you the first consequences of our discovery. Indeed, the text of the tablets was long enough that, thanks to the invaluable collaboration of Yves Duguy, we were able to establish the rules for deciphering Linear A. The technical details of this remarkable achievement will be presented shortly, but I first want to explain why these documents reveal so much about the Minoans. They have the same author, in this case a woman. The tablets constitute what she herself calls her will, while the second ones contain her memoirs. She dictated her will to two scribes, one for each language, with the mission of copying it and ensuring that every household in Crete had a copy in its language. In contrast, she wrote the papyri herself, totalling more than 60 meters of text of remarkable quality. Reading these memoirs allowed us, as I announced in my email, to reconstruct the history of the Minoans almost in its entirety. Of course, we lack information on what happened after the author's death, but you will see that she anticipated what was to come."

"So far, we have only focused on deciphering Linear A and translating the papyri and tablets. You now hold printouts of the complete versions of both documents. I won't reveal their contents here: it would take too long, and it would be a shame to deprive you of the joy of discovering them for yourselves. In the future, specialists will study these texts and their implications for our understanding of Minoan civilisation. To whet your appetite, I can already share a few names you'll need to familiarise yourselves with. First, you'll no longer call them Minoans but Hattianteans, as that's the name they gave themselves. Additionally, as you already know, we are not on the island of Santorini but on Hattiarina. Its main city, revealed by Spyridon Marinatos's excavations at Akrotiri, was called Urukinea, meaning the new Uruk."

Aristotle pauses to allow the astonishment created by this reference to the city of ancient Mesopotamia to pass.

"I won't say more on that for now. In the translations, we've used the Hattiantean names for cities rather than the Greek names of current excavation sites. At the beginning of the memoirs, you'll find maps and correspondence tables to help you navigate."

"One last point before Yves Duguy takes the floor to explain the fascinating process of deciphering Linear A. The texts tell us that each Minoan city was ruled by a woman whose title we have had difficulty translating because we also did not know the corresponding term written on the Linear B tablet. She wasn't a queen or priestess, as those terms are familiar in archaic Greek. Reading the memoirs, we understood she was essentially a moral authority recognised by all. She does not intervene directly in the administration of the city, which is ensured by a person qualified as General Intendant. On the other hand, she alone assumes the exercise of justice. We ultimately chose the term Matriarch, particularly because people addressed her as "Mother"".

"That's all for now. I pass the microphone to Yves, who will explain our discoveries on Linear A far better than I could."

§

Toponyms

Correspondence of the names of the places mentioned in the memoirs:

Islands

Hattiarina: Santorini (Thera)

Kephti: Crete

Sukipawu: Cyprus

Hattiantean (Minoan) cities

Urukinea: Akrotiri archaeological site in Santorini

Kunisuu: Knossos

Kamaljia: archaeological site of Malia

Gurnjia: Gournia

Dikta: Palaikastro

Kalataa: Galatas (Archaeological Site of Galatas-Arkalochori)

Vatypetawa: archaeological site of Vathypetro

Turusa: Tylisos

Gortunjia: Gortyn

Mesaraa: Messara

Payto: archaeological site of Phaistos

Opsjia: archaeological site of Monastiraki

Dawo: archaeological site of Aghia Triada

Kommo: archaeological site of Kommo

Dawrometo: Rethymno

Summit

Psilowitis: Psiloritis (Mount Ida)

Units of measure

1 inch: about 3 cm (1.2 inch)

1 cubit: about 35 cm (1.1 foot)

1 stadium: about 300 m (330 yards)

1 lead: 0.5 kg (1.1 lb)

Maps

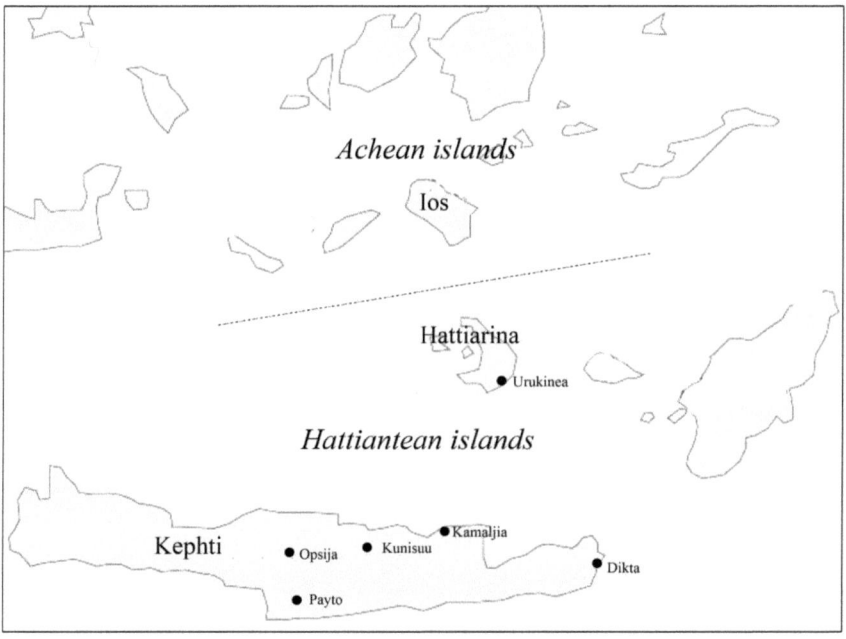

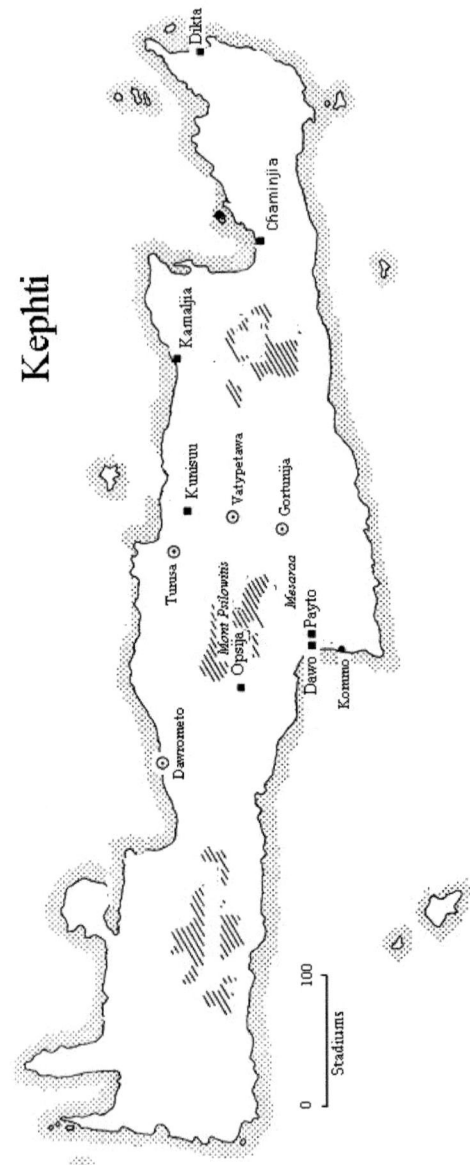

THEODOSSIS

I am writing here my memories of the time when the Hattiantean people lived in peace and harmony on the magnificent islands of Hattiarina and Kephti, as well as of the time when immense misfortunes befell them, which they fought against with all their might.

§

I was born in Urukinea, a city on the island of Hattiarina, on the sixth day of the second month in the 982nd year of the Hattiantean foundation. My parents named me Asiraa. My father was a fisherman. He died at sea when I was seven. My mother, my younger brother Adikete, and I lived with my uncle. We were like siblings with our two cousins, Isthar and Ninlil, and their brother Noda. My mother taught writing at Urukinea's school. She taught me to write and count very early. Thanks to her, I joined the school of architecture at thirteen. My interest in this art came from the clay models displayed in front of houses under construction. Once the work site was completed, they were thrown away with the rubble. I collected them and, little by little, I recreated a miniature village in the basement of our house. My cousins and I each had our own houses, painted in our colours to avoid confusion.

A colleague of my mother, a teacher of drawing and painting, often visited our house. He was in love with her and, perhaps to have an excuse to visit, offered to give me lessons. That's how our home became the most decorated in the city. I started with the girls' bedroom. I sketched a design, and while my cousins coloured the flowers and the trees, I painted my favourite animals. Once our room was fully decorated, we moved on to the hallway and, step by step, almost every wall in the house was covered. It felt like we lived among animals all day long. My mother's lover told everyone about it, earning me the nickname of "the little girl who paints frescoes". People even came to visit our house.

At the school of architecture, we spent a lot of time on construction sites. It was during one of them that I first met Mother Inanna, the Matriarch of Hattiarina. I was plastering the façade of a building in a new neighbourhood outside Urukinea. She came with the craftsmen, architects, and Quarter Intendants to inspect the progress. As she walked down our street, we all stopped to watch the event from the top of our scaffolding. She was going from house to house, questioning the foremen and talking to the workers. When she passed by our site, she recognised me.

"Asiraa! I stopped by your house this morning. I wanted to talk to you. Could you come down, please?"

Since I was little, I have admired our Matriarch. I found her very beautiful and envied her imposing height, which commanded respect. Unfortunately, our first meeting was not as I had imagined. With my mason's smock too large and covered in dust I looked like a clay pot. She smiled at me and then, after complimenting me on the plaster on my wall, she ran her hand through my hair to dust it.

"We're alike, you and I: we both have plenty of white hair, though not for the same reasons, sadly! … As I mentioned, I'd like to speak with you. Could you come and see me at the Central House? Tomorrow, at the tenth hour, if that suits you."

I couldn't believe it. Of course it suited me.

§

My mother was redoing my bun for the third time. She thought the curled strands sticking out weren't long enough.

"You'll put your cousin's new dress on. You never have anything decent to wear. With a few adjustments, it'll fit you just fine. I need to do your nails—they're a mess. You'll wear my large earrings and the gold necklace your father gave me. And, for once, you'll put makeup on. You can't go looking like that; people won't even know if you're a boy or a girl."

At that time in Urukinea, Egyptian-style makeup was fashionable. All the boys and girls wanted to look like the princes and princesses depicted on the papyri, embroideries, and vases brought back by merchants. I didn't like wearing makeup. I thought it took too much time for a look that always faded throughout the day.

During these preparations, the question that had kept me awake all night haunted me: what did Mother Inanna want to tell me? I tried to recall anything I had done or said that might explain her request, but by the time I was ready to leave, I had no answers. Groomed and manicured by my mother, made up and dressed by my cousin, for once, I thought I looked rather pretty. Of course, it was impossible to prevent the whole family from accompanying me. Surrounded by this excited procession, dressed as ever, I felt ridiculous. But I didn't care: I had a meeting with the Matriarch.

Arriving at the Central House, the question of what Mother Inanna had to ask me returned, accompanied with the anguish caused by the sight of the entrance porch. I tried to gather my thoughts, but my uncle had already announced our arrival to the usher, who gestured for us to follow him. After escorting my "suite" to a modestly decorated room, he led me directly to the Matriarch.

Her office, located on the top floor, was bright and spacious, but I was surprised by its lack of decoration. The only embellishment was a vine motif that ran around the room near the ceiling. While the design was lovely, it left the walls bare and rather austere. Sitting at a table, Mother Inanna was reading a papyrus. Standing beside her, I recognised the General Intendant. She looked up.

"Ah! Our little girl who paints frescoes. I'll be with you in just a moment."

Maybe she wanted to ask me to decorate her office? As she continued her conversation with the General Intendant, I began imagining what I could paint to give her the most beautiful office in the city. She handed the papyrus to the Intendant. He withdrew.

"Asiraa! You look stunning! I'm flattered that you came so prepared to come see me. You're radiant."

Unlike me, she was dressed very simply. Her hair tied back in a ponytail, with only little makeup, she wore a plain gray dress tied at the waist with a simple rope. I felt like I was in costume.

"As I mentioned yesterday, I have something important to ask you. There's no rush. You can take all the time you need to respond. But first, remind me: how old are you?"

"I'll be seventeen soon, Mother."

"You must be one of the youngest at the school of architecture."

"I am the youngest in the fourth year. Thanks to my mother, who is a teacher."

"Thanks to your talents too, don't you think?"

"Maybe…"

"Your mother certainly thinks so. I can tell you she's proud of you."

My mother, proud of me! For sure, it was the first time I heard that.

"Let's get to my question. I'm forty-eight years old. You know that, according to our tradition, the Matriarch must name her successor by her fiftieth year at the latest."

A lump formed in my stomach. I tried to say, "Yes, I know" but no words came out.

"I've been fortunate to enjoy good health, so I've postponed this obligation until now. But the time has come. As is customary, I've done my research."

The lump in my stomach was growing.

"Everyone in the city knows the little girl who paints frescoes. They think you're very talented and like you a lot. But if you're here, it's mainly because I've also spoken to your teachers. They appreciate you. Do you know you impress them?"

I felt tears welling up.

"I believe that you have understood. Yes, it's to you I would like to ask if you would accept being my successor."

Everything was mixing up. Pride, fear, the desire to flee and even the ridiculous worry that my tears would cause my makeup to run.

"If you accept, you'll spend several years apprenticing with me. You'll attend council meetings, and most importantly, I'll teach you how to render justice."

I was fixing my gaze on the frieze above her.

"It will require a lot of work on top of your studies. Take your time. Think about whether you would enjoy organizing the city, helping people resolve disputes, and judging those who

behave badly. It's a challenging and demanding role. If you feel it's not for you, tell me without fear."
She added, looking directly into my eyes:
"Personally, I am sure of you."
I managed to smile.
"Take your time and come back to see me whenever you'd like to discuss this."

§

On the way back, clutching my mother's arm, my bun undone to hide in my hair, I couldn't stop crying. I thought about what Mother Inanna had told me, about my running makeup, about the sad walls of the office, everything made me cry. No one said a word, except Adikete, who kept repeating:
"What's wrong with Asi? Why is she crying?"
Thankfully, I had my construction work. I returned to the site the very next day. My foreman was a kind but very demanding man. He would check everything and made us redo our work without hesitation if it wasn't perfect. That was exactly what I needed to clear my mind. No house in Hattiarina ever had a wall plastered as perfectly as mine.
Little by little, I got used to the idea. I could think about the question without bursting into tears. Unfortunately, I realised I had no idea what a Matriarch's day-to-day life entailed. So I tried to talk about it with those around me. Isthar immediately saw the appeal of being the Matriarch's cousin. She declared herself the "Chief advisor in charge of

festivities." Every evening, she would come up with new ideas for festivities, games, or performances. They sometimes lacked realism, they always were very cheerful, each time it ended in fits of laughter, but that didn't help me at all. For her part, my mother could not imagine that I might refuse. Whenever I tried to share my doubts, she would get upset, forcing me to end the conversation. Our relationship had always been strained. Sometimes, it felt like she didn't trust me, or even that she was afraid of me. We couldn't talk normally. Whenever we disagreed about something, it turned into a drama.

Yet it was her attitude that helped me out of my indecision. Since I returned to work at architecture school, I realised how much this profession captivated me. Even if I found it difficult imagining what a Matriarch did, I knew it would force me to abandon it. My indecision was more due to fear of my mother's reaction than to any hesitation on my part. Involuntarily, she helped me becoming aware of what I really wanted. Determined to follow only my own aspirations, I asked for an audience with Mother Innana.

When I entered her office, I was not overconfident. I prepared myself for anger or, worse, disappointment. But she showed none of that. She listened attentively, then confided that she wasn't surprised, having noticed how much pleasure I was taking in my studies. After a long conversation that stretched into the evening, she made one final suggestion as we parted: "Your decision might not be fully informed. Would you agree to go and see for yourself? You could intern in different city departments and meet the people who work there. What do you think?"

I was sure of myself but I didn't have the courage to refuse her once again.

After this hectic period, I organised myself as best I could between my classes, my construction sites and the internships in town, which allowed me to resume my usual routine: building crooked walls, painting frescoes in every free corner of our house, enraging the boys who were chasing us, and leaving in fits of laughter with Isthar.

§

My first internship at the Central House involved tallying delivered goods and services. It was easy and dull, so that Mother Inanna sent me to Aphaia, the port of Urukinea. The climate there was very different. Organised around a square extending into two quays, one for receipts and the other for dispatches, it was a hive of constant activity. To the north, a large covered hall housed counters where goods were inspected and recorded. Strong men, almost naked, carried items between boats and warehouses. The square teemed with idle sailors waiting for their captains to finish with formalities. Opposite the piers, the awnings of the taverns were overgrown with pink and white clematis. All the languages of the world mixed together in a din of invectives and bursts of laughter.

I was supposed to begin by handling the records at the counters. However, due to a sudden death, they needed someone who spoke Achaean for trade negotiations. My mother had insisted I learn that language, claiming it would be useful someday. My supervisor had hastily taught me the rules but had not explained the negotiation process in detail. He only warned me that, in general, Achaeans didn't like the Hattianteans, whom they accused of thinking they were the centre of the world. Actually, my first client encounter was anything but smooth. Panos, a wool merchant, was from Ios, an Achaean island located north of Hattiarina, half a day's sail away. After a moment of surprise upon entering the office, he explained to me that, given the importance of his affairs, there could be no question of him handling them with an intern. Before the interview, I was afraid of not knowing how to behave. The condescending tone he used when he said "an intern" set my mind straight. I told him that I could understand the discomfort caused by this unforeseen change, but that, knowing his file well, I would be able to respect his interests. He insisted, demanding to see my superior. I told him that he had appointed me to deal with him and that I saw no reason to disturb him. Panos grew angry and called me a "little conceited black head." One did not know where this nickname "black heads" that the Achaeans gave us came from, but nobody was unaware of what it expressed. Conceited might have passed, but "black head" was too much. I told him that I was not going to be able to let his goods in and I left without giving him time to respond. He remained stunned for a moment, then ran into the hallway to apologise. We calmly returned to the office to discuss what he wanted in exchange for his 1,200 mines of wool. Later, I learned that my supervisor, knowing Panos's fiery temper, had assigned him to me "for training."

After that lively introduction, our relationship improved significantly. He was an honest and straightforward man with whom I enjoyed negotiating, and I knew the feeling was mutual. Once our business was settled, we often chatted about other things. In fact, it was mainly him who talked about his life. Originally a fisherman in Naxos, he often stopped in Aphaia during his fishing trips. After frequenting the port's taverns, he realised that Hattiarina, with its limited pastures, lacked wool. He converted his fishing boat for trade and settled in Ios, closer to Hattiarina. He collected the finest wool from the Achaean islands and exchanged it in Hattiarina for bronze and earthenware, which were renowned for their quality among the Achaeans. This trade had made him, in his words, one of the wealthiest merchants in Ios.

He often spoke of his son, Theodossis, a boy full of promise whom he intended to introduce to me since, one day, I'd have to deal with him instead. No matter how much I explained that I would soon leave the trade office, he insisted. Each time, he promised to bring him on his next trip, but each time, something came up. I began to wonder if this prodigal son even existed. It was only on the last day of my internship that he finally came accompanied by the young man. Young—and mostly very handsome. Tanned skin, curly brown hair, he was the complete opposite of the Hattiantean beauty ideals, but I found him very handsome. Plus, something unknown to us, he had blue eyes! While I was negotiating the value of a mine of wool with his father, I looked at him out of the corner of my eye. He was staring at me with an expression somewhere between astonished and captivated. When it was time to part, he stammered, "See you soon". My internship at the trade office was over, so the chances of meeting him again were poor.

§

Back at my studies, I reconnected with my friends from the school of architecture and, for the most part, forgot about the handsome Achaean. Not entirely, though, as evidenced by the pang in my chest whenever something reminded me of our brief encounter. One evening, while celebrating a classmate's graduation in a tavern at the port, I spotted him walking in front of the terraces, lost in thought. I rushed toward him, shouting and waving my arms.
"Hey, Achaean! Remember me? From the warehouses, with your father."
"Of course, I remember you. I hoped to see you again, but each time, someone else received us."
"I don't work there any more."
We were smiling foolishly at each other, eye to eye. His father arrived, out of breath.
"Ah! There you are. I've been … "

His gaze shifted between us, back and forth.

"... looking all over for you. Excuse us, Asiraa, but we must set board immediately. It's late."

My classmates had clearly seen what had happened. Jokes began to spring. Upset, I couldn't react to their banters. I left the table, ignoring their apologies.

In the days that followed, my primary concern was figuring out how to see him again. Between my construction work, architecture classes, and city internships, I had no time to visit the port. I asked a friend who worked there to let me know as soon as she saw him. I knew I could trust her discretion: my classmates' gossip had spread a rumour about my "affair" with an Achaean, which had already reached my mother's ears.

A few weeks later, a young Egyptian brought me a scrap of papyrus scribbled on by my friend. Theodossis was at the quay on his boat. As I was leaving, pretending to have a family issue, my foreman said to me mockingly:

"And... it is normal that you to keep your smock full of plaster on you."

No one had ever been as fast as me to get to Aphaia, without running and keeping a normal air. When I reached his boat, he was busy coiling ropes, unaware of my presence.

"Will you take me for a sail?" I called out.

He looked up, startled, as if to say, "What does that girl want from me?"

Then, nearly tripping over the ropes, he leapt onto the dock.

"Get aboard. We're leaving now."

Unaware of my complete lack of sailing knowledge, he began barking orders at me in Achaean, using technical terms I didn't understand. I tried to improvise, pretending to know what I was doing, but it didn't work. The more mistakes I made, the more irritated he became and the more I laughed. Finally, dejected, he did the manoeuvre all by himself after ordering me to sit in the middle and not to touch anything.

Carried by a light breeze from the overheated land, we sailed along the coast, past the famous red, white, and black cliffs of Aphaia, renowned throughout Hattiarina. Sitting on a net, my head resting on his thigh, I enjoyed the warmth of the sun on my skin and especially the pleasure of the contact with his. I waited for him to stop the boat, pull me close, and kiss me. Unfortunately, when we reached the western tip, the open sea's strong wind and choppy waves forced us to turn back. Soaked by the spray, we had no choice but to return as quickly as possible. Disappointed and shivery with cold, I had to settle for huddling against him.

We returned to port at nightfall. Sheltered from the wind, the air was still mild. Lying between his legs, I watched the sky, waiting for a shooting star. He pulled me up to his height and —finally—kissed me. Then he rolled onto me, his hands exploring my body, first over my clothes, then underneath. On the dock, I could hear people talking and laughing. I was afraid they would see us. With awkward twists and muffled giggles, we slipped under a sail and made love silently, gently, for a long time. Completely content, I wished I could stay there, trapped beneath his weight, forever.

When I arrived home, I worried my mother might still be awake, waiting for me. She was asleep. The next morning, she had her face from the days when she ruminated on her bad mood. As I was about to leave, she couldn't hold back any longer.

"Where were you last night?"

"I stayed at the port with friends from school."

"You could have let us know you'd be home late."

"It was decided just like that. It was not planned."

She shrugged her shoulders.

§

In Hattiarina, any excuse was good enough for a celebration. These included major historical events, like the founding of Urukinea or the creation of the Grand Federation of Cities, as well as seasonal cycles. We were approaching the summer solstice. On this occasion, everyone gathered on the hill overlooking Urukinea to watch the sun set over the sea. Once it had disappeared, we would return to the city for a shared meal. The festivities would continue all night at dances and taverns scattered throughout the city. At dawn, we all would climb back to the hill to watch the sun rise from the opposite side and confirm it was indeed the solstice, thanks to an upright stone pierced with a hole. As the sun appeared, its light passed through the hole to form a glowing spot on the wall opposite. Though predictable, the event always drew cheers and applause. I wanted to share this celebration with Theodossis.

The path to the hill was packed with people. My mother was with the painting teacher, and my uncle, having indulged in some white wine at home, was acting very affectionate toward his wife. Everybody had his mind elsewhere, which suited me well. Once the sun had set, we descended to Urukinea for the banquet. Tables were set up in every square, where anyone could sit and serve themselves from enormous pots simmering nearby. We joined the painting teacher and his family at their table. A multitude of children were running all over the place, delighted that no one was taking care of them any more. My little cousin, my brother and her cousin were playing hide and seek in our legs, uttering shrill screams. It reminded me painfully of when I used to do the same, ending up on my father's lap, cuddled close to avoid being caught.

My uncle tried to talk boating with Theodossis but, each knowing only a few words of the other's language and, with the racket that echoed in the square, their conversation was cut short. My mother only had eyes for the painting teacher. Isthar started by sulking because her father had forced her to stay with us, then, without anyone noticing, she disappeared. After the meal, as people left the tables to stretch or recline on patches of grass, space was made for dancing. Theodossis and I strolled between squares, watching others dance before heading to his boat to make love. For the first time, I didn't watch the sun rise on the morning of the solstice.

§

Theodossis left at first light. Before heading to class, I stopped home to change. The little ones were still asleep. My mother was cleaning. She barely greeted me.
"You could have come with us to see the sunrise."
"Theodossis wanted to leave early. He needed to be in Naxos before noon."
"Isthar didn't come either. Her father is furious. She just got back."
"She's at that age, isn't she?"
"She's following her cousin's example."
Exhausted, I wanted at all costs to avoid the confrontation my mother was looking for. I left immediately for architecture school.
That evening, the ambiance at home was still tense. The boys played silently, and Isthar was crying in our room. At dinner, no one spoke. Even Adikete kept his eyes fixed on his plate. Finally, on edge, I spoke up.
"I don't understand. Last night, we were all happy to be together. Why not now any more?"
After a long silence, my uncle responded.
"If you were so happy with us, then why didn't you join us on the hill this morning?"
"I can't believe it's because of that you're in this mood!"
My mother exploded.

"It is, actually! What do you hope with this Achaean? The entire city noticed your absence. Let me remind you: you're not just anyone. Do you think Mother Inanna will accept a girl who stops out with an Achaean? She'll revoke her decision, and we'll be disgraced!"

"That's what bothers you, isn't it? You won't be the mother of the future Matriarch any more. You won't get to walk the streets, giving knowing smiles to people. You won't get to brag to your friends about being received at the Central House. That's all you care about. You only think of yourself."

My uncle slammed his fist on the table, startling everyone.

"That's enough! You and your cousin are insufferable. Leave the table!"

He frightened me. Until then, he had never intervened between my mother and me but, exasperated by Isthar's nocturnal escapade, he could not hold back. I was shaking like a leaf.

From the bedroom, Isthar had heard his father scream. She explained to me that, during the banquet, she had slipped away to meet a boy who said he was in love with her. She didn't feel in love with him, but he kept trying to kiss her and she wanted to know what it felt like. They had gone into hiding during the sunset to "practice." She hadn't enjoyed it much but had been curious to try more. She made me laugh a lot telling me about the adventures that followed. Pleased with herself, she declared it had been worthwhile and fell asleep. Whimsical, mischievous, daredevil, she was the complete opposite of me and yet we were going along like twins.

I spent the rest of the night mulling over what had happened since the interview with Mother Inanna: the arguments with my mother, the moments of happiness with Theodossis, the reproachful looks in the street, the anger of my uncle. Mother Inanna had turned my life upside down by trying to link my destiny to that of the city. This wasn't what I wanted. I wanted to live with Theodossis and build beautiful houses in which people would be happy. As dawn broke, I finally fell asleep, resolved to tell both Mother Inanna and my own mother about my decision.

§

Adikete was shaking me roughly. It took me a moment to wake up from this very short night and realise that I was going to be late. I threw on whatever I could find and dashed out without even seeing my mother. As I reached the square in front of the school of architecture, reflecting on how I would speak to Mother Inanna, a violent tremor shook the ground beneath me, throwing me off balance and sending a woman near me to the ground. A dull rumble was coming from below, from everywhere. The earth started trembling. The ground was undulating and carrying us right and left. People were rushing outside screaming, running in all directions looking for a place where the earth wouldn't shake. In the houses, we could hear the crash of tumbling dishes and collapsing ceilings. The lintel of the school porch broke in two, causing a section of wall above it to fall down. It felt endless. A fear of death, of the end of the world, was paralysing me. Then the tremors subsided. The roar faded away. There was only a cloud of dust left, floating above the ground. People stopped moving, worried to see if it wouldn't start again. Groups began forming. They told each other how they felt, arguing about how long it had lasted. No one dared to return to the houses. Terrified, the children remained clinging to their parents. A man was sitting on the ground, haggard, his head bleeding. A woman was screaming, asking for help for her injured child. Little by little, people organised themselves. Some cleared the bulkiest rubble, while others helped injured people.

I entered the school to see if there was any further damage. Very old, the buildings had been the subject of successive patch up jobs, not always carried out according to the rules of the art. The whole thing had held up poorly. Some rooms were completely unusable. A student was seriously injured when a ceiling collapsed. Fortunately, those who did not have time to go out into the street were able to take refuge in the courtyard. There was rubble everywhere. As I was discussing the situation with my classmates, a messenger from the Central House called out to me. Mother Inanna had urgently summoned all the Quarter Intendants and she thought it would be a good opportunity to make me understand the role of a Matriarch.

§

At the Central House, the damage was limited: a few sheets of wall plaster peeled off, broken terracotta everywhere and some dislodged flagstones. In the city, the situation was chaotic. The Intendants had only fragmentary information about the injured and the damage. No deaths had been reported. At this hour of day, everyone had had time to get out at the first shake. At first glance, most buildings seemed to have withstood the tremor. The General Intendant was especially concerned about the state of the ducts networks. He feared sewers might be blocked. Mother Inanna distributed the tasks so that we could quickly get into action. The most urgent were the injured, the water distribution network and the sewers. Next, it was necessary to assess the condition of the streets and roads, mainly the one leading to Aphaia. Mother Inanna entrusted me to visit the homes in order to identify their difficulties and check the safety of the buildings. The next council meeting was scheduled for the following evening.

Before beginning my assignment, I stopped by home to check on my family and let them know I was safe. Everyone was unharmed. The worst casualty was the fresco in the boys' room. The giant red and yellow octopus had mostly crumbled to the ground. On the wall, all that remained were a few tentacle tips and a solitary eye. I promised Adikete I would renovate it. I suggested that he gathers the pieces and put the octopus back together so that I could copy it again. He liked the idea and got started immediately. Despite the late hour, I returned to the school to form a survey team. Everyone was busy clearing rubble and preparing for repairs, but I managed to recruit two girls and a boy. Together, we devised a plan: ask households about injuries and daily challenges, then conduct a thorough inspection of their homes' structural integrity.

People were reassured by our quick arrival. Often, they had to clear space for us to sit amidst the debris. They started by sharing their material concerns related to the earthquake, which were often similar: Were the food stores damaged? When would they reopen? How to dispose of the rubble? How to calm and occupy the children? After these material concerns, the conversation became more familiar, to the point of telling anecdotes like a grandmother who had been found all white, covered in dust, or a kid who found it very amusing that the earth made him dance. The older ones recalled their memories of the earthquake which, forty years earlier, had destroyed an entire neighbourhood. Unlike my previous administrative internships, I enjoyed this mission. It allowed me to meet a variety of people, understand their concerns, comfort them, and provide helpful advice.

§

At the time of the earthquake, Theodossis was on a tour of the Northern Isles bringing back hides and bales of goat's wool. Alarmed by the damage at the port, he immediately set out to find me. After checking the school, he located me in the neighbourhood where I was conducting surveys. For three days, I had been visiting homes from morning to night. What a joy to see him as I left the last house of the day! I let out a shrill cry and threw myself at him, drawing the attention of passers-by. I didn't care and even it gave me an idea. Having finished the day's survey, I had to return to school where we collected our notes. The inn across the street where all the students used to meet had just reopened. I was sure to find some friends there. As we entered, the noise level dipped. Two of my friends were seated with beers in hand.

"Can we join you?"

Their awkward expressions almost made me laugh, but I maintained a nonchalant demeanour.

"I don't need to introduce Theodossis, do I? I'm dropping off my notes at the school and will be right back."

Ignoring Theodossis's panicked look, I left quickly before they could react.

Prejudices only feed on preconceived ideas. Faced with reality, they disappear on their own. Theodossis told me that, after an initially tense silence, they were forced to engage in conversation. One of them, who spoke a little Achaean, owned a boat and regularly participated in regattas on Hattiarina inner sea. Theodossis was of a nature of few words, except when it came to navigation techniques. Between the two of them, the discussion quickly became very lively on the comparative performance of Egyptian, Hattiantean and

Achaean sails. They promised each other, on occasion, to meet again at the port to talk about it again on the boats.

Strengthened by this first result, I decided to take Theodossis home to provoke a discussion with my mother and my uncle. When we arrived home, they had not yet returned. Adikete was working on his mosaic of octopus. He immediately requisitioned Theodossis. Lying on the bed, tired from a day spent listening to people, I happily watched them argue about the location of the pieces of fresco.

When my mother entered the room, I had fallen asleep. Theodossis and Adikete were still working on the mosaic. She woke me with a curt "Good evening!" directed at no one. Ostensibly ignoring Theodossis, she dragged me into the living room "to talk to me", that is to say to blow up at me. Outside of herself, she held back her voice so that Theodossis would not hear. After calling me a fool sacrificing her future for a romance with a stranger, she ended up telling me that if I didn't want to devote myself to my future as a Matriarch all I had to do was leave the house and go with my Achaean. It was too much. I returned to the room where Theodossis and Adikete had obviously heard our argument.

"Let's go! We're leaving."

"Where?"

"I don't know. But I can't stay here another minute."

Adikete clung to me.

"I don't want you to leave! I want you to stay—with Theodossis."

He wrapped himself around my waist.

"Don't worry. I'll come back. Do you think I could leave my darling Adikete behind? "

Theodossis managed to calm him by promising that he, too, would return to finish the mosaic with him. Once we were out of the house, Theodossis asked:

"What happened? What did your mother say?"

"No matter. I don't want to have to stand her reprimands any more."

"Where will you go?"

"I don't know. I'll ask my friend in Aphaia if I can stay with her for a few days. After that, I'll figure it out."

"I think you're exhausted. You need some time to yourself. I have an idea. Every year, my friends and I take a wild retreat to an isolated beach on Ios. If you'd like, I'll take you there and invite them to join us. I'm sure they'll be thrilled."

It was true that, since the earthquake, between council meetings, inquiries among residents and my mother's moods, I had been on edge. Finding myself far from all that, with nothing else to do than laze on a beach in the shade of tamarisk trees and enjoy Theodossis, I couldn't hope for better. I just took the time to complete my surveys while Theodossis lent a hand to the port where the damage was significant, and four days later, we set sail for Ios.

§

THE EXPLOSION

The arrival in Ios was via a harbour at the bottom of which the houses of the port stood out. They were all bright white, unlike ours, always decorated with colourful geometric patterns. Among these, Theodossis was soon able to show me his father's. Rather than living in the city set back on the plain, Panos had preferred to settle just above the harbour, to continue to hear it live and to enjoy the sunsets. Despite the unexpected nature of our visit, Theodossis' parents welcomed us warmly, without asking any questions. Their daughter Penelope and her companion Mikis came to join us for the evening meal. From the terrace, we could hear the noise of the taverns and, on the harbour, the reflection of the moon was scattered in a myriad of candles.

Panos animated the evening all by himself. He began by telling about our meeting in Aphaia and our outbursts. He kept adding more and more, but he made us laugh so much that I ensured to hold back from re-establishing the truth. He peppered his tales with stories that the Achaeans told themselves about us. In addition to being proud, we were formidable traders capable of fooling any Achaean. He had the same for the Egyptians, credited with a naivety bordering on stupidity. I was not very much for on those kinds of jokes, but told by Panos at the end of a meal with plenty to drink, I had a stomach ache from laughing.

The next day, Theodossis went around to his friends to recruit those who were available. In the afternoon, loaded like donkeys, we embarked, me, Penelope and Mikis on Theodossis' boat, two boys and two girls on another boat. As usual, I did everything wrong for the departure manoeuvre and Theodossis got angry (we had almost rammed a fishing boat). He argued with his sister who asked him to calm down so that half the trip passed in silence. Fortunately, Mikis had the good idea to offer to take the helm. I was able to reconcile with Theodossis and convince him to go and do the same with his sister.

The cove where we landed was only an hour's sail away. It had two small sandy beaches separated by rocks. From one escapade to another, Theodossis and his friends had built shelters there to sleep and, on a rock, a covered terrace with a table and chairs. It was already very hot. As soon as the equipment was unloaded and stored in the shade, we all undressed to jump into the water. After this first invigorating bath, things got organised. Two girls went to explore the beaches and the edges of the cove in search of dead wood. Mikis set up the fire pit with large stones around a hollow in the sand, another boy cleared a water hole between rocks to place the jars of wine and water, and Theodossis went fishing.

Penelope and I were assigned to prepare the evening meal, which, as far as I was concerned, was not the best choice. Once all that was in place, all we had to do was lounge around, swim, eat, sing, laugh and make love.

Near the spring where we used to go to get water, there was some fairly good clay, without too many inclusions. To occupy the hot afternoon hours, I undertook to make the model of our future house. I knew where I wanted to build it: on a hill outside Urukinea from where the view towards the plains and the sea was magnificent. We were more or less in agreement on the layout: a large half-covered terrace to be able to receive our friends, our bedroom open to the east to have the sun in the morning, a beautiful living room decorated with frescoes, an office for me where I could draw my plans, and above all an ice silo to cool the house in the summer. The only subject of discord was the number of bedrooms, that is to say, the number of children. He wanted two or three, I at least six or seven. Considering that it was premature to argue about this subject, I settled the matter by making only one room, arranged in such a way that it would be easy to add others. Then I made figurines to represent us. The difficulty was our skin colours. His was coppery, especially in the sun, while mine was white. One day, I told him that he was the colour of onion skin. I found it pretty, but he did not appreciate the vegetable image. To get revenge, he compared me to a turnip, which I did not like at all. Since the clay was white, to make Theodossis, I had to add shell powder. For our children, I prudently limited myself to two, one "onion skin" and one "turnip".

§

In the evening we used to stay around the fire until very late and often they would ask me questions about the Hattianteans. Many things about us intrigued them. I then told them the story of our founding.

"We come from the country of Warka, a distant land where the plains, as vast and fertile as those of Egypt, shelter the city of Uruk. It has prospered there for centuries, but it is constantly at war because its wealth arouses the covetousness of neighbouring cities. For this reason, a thousand years ago, Nanaya, queen of Uruk, sent three of her most valiant knights looking for a land where she could found a new city and live there in peace forever. They went up the country of Warka towards the north. They crossed the country of Akkad, the country of Assur, the country of Mitanni, but all were equally ravaged by wars. So, they came back and told the queen that war was everywhere and that there was no place to live in peace. Queen Nanaya would not listen. She sent them away, ordering them to go further and not return until they had found it."

"They set out again beyond the land of Mitanni, to the land of Arzawa, where they arrived at the city of Millawanda, on the shores of our sea. They had still not seen a land at peace. They were despairing of being able to satisfy their queen when a fisherman from Millawanda told them of an island that was said to be very fertile and which had been abandoned by its inhabitants for an unknown reason. It was called Hattiarina, which meant "the crescent moon island". Then one of the knights said: "An island will keep us away from wars. Let us go and see it." They saw the great plains sloping gently towards the sea, the cedar forests, the water that flowed abundantly from the mountain, the deep and sheltered harbour where a port could be built. They returned to Uruk, certain that their queen would be satisfied."

"Queen Nanaya gathered the best craftsmen, the best scribes, the best architects, the best astronomers, the best in all the trades that a city needs. She asked them to leave with her to found a new city in Hattiarina. They all loved her and they all wanted her to remain their queen. She abdicated in favor of her brother and they left with her. This is how Queen Nanaya founded the city of Urukinea and, in less than two years, all the Hattianteans cities will celebrate the first millennium of this foundation!"

"They say you have no king or queen." said Mikis.

"That is true. Kings should govern for the good of their people. Unfortunately, they themselves are governed by their personal ambitions and forget this duty. Queen Nanaya wanted to put an end to the power struggles that constantly agitated Uruk and its neighbours. She decided that her people would not be governed by individuals but by moral principles accepted and applied by everyone. Since then, we have neither king, nor queen, nor priests nor priestesses."

Penelope became the voice of all the others:

"But how is life organised in your cities if you don't have a king to rule over it?"

"What governs the Hattianteans is their personal conscience and the morality that Queen Nanaya taught us. It is engraved on a marble stela sealed at the entrance of each Central House:

- Unless he threatens you, do not inflict on anyone anything that you would not want inflicted on you;
- Value other people as much as you value yourself;
- Do not disturb the natural order and do not attempt to take life unless it is necessary for your own.

For ten centuries, these precepts have governed our daily lives."

"Is that all?"

"To be followed, laws must be known. Everyone can easily remember these three rules. They are taught to the Hattianteans from a young age. If you study them, you will see that each of our actions can be evaluated in relation to one of them. In order to guarantee their harmonious application, each Hattiantean city is under the moral authority of a woman to whom everyone can refer. We call her "Mother" because she has the same role as a mother towards her children: she guides us while letting us choose our own path. She only exercises her authority to settle disputes when the parties cannot reach an agreement."

They couldn't believe it. In Ios, their city was ruled by a governor who exercised power over the entire island, himself subject to the authority of the king of Mycenae. Mikis intervened.

"And who puts people in prison?"

"In our country, as anywhere else, some people behave badly. Those around them first try to reason with them and help them to change their behaviour. Anyone who persists in outraging our morals is judged by the Matriarch, who can impose reparations or even banish him from the Hattiantean lands. But we do not have prisons. Locking someone in a dungeon would be contrary to our first principle. Only those who represent an immediate threat are locked up awaiting judgment by the Matriarch."

Despite Theodossis' efforts to convince them, they remained incredulous. They could not imagine a people who were not under the authority of a sovereign.

§

Accustomed to the morning light, we were waking up later and later. On the sixth day, however, I woke up at dawn, seized by a worry that I did not understand. Suddenly, there was an immense blinding light that woke the others too. We were wondering what had happened when a detonation shook the ground, continuing into a roll of thunder such as we had never heard. An intense pain pierced our ears. We rushed to the beach. Standing out against the still pale sky, a gigantic column of black smoke was rising at full speed above Hattiarina. At the base of the cloud, fireballs formed and then swirled upward into the smoke. The explosions followed one another without stopping. Furrowed with flashes of lightning, the column of smoke rose to a vertiginous height. Terrifying, fascinating, it seemed unreal. I screamed:

"My mother, Adikete, Isthar, they are all there. Let's go and rescue them!"

With his eyes, Theodossis was trying to convince me that it was not possible.

"They will die. We have to go get them. Take me. Quickly!"

As we were pushing the boat afloat, our panicked comrades hurriedly gathered their belongings to return to port. I don't know how, but for once I executed all the manoeuvres of setting sail without making a mistake. At sea, I couldn't help but position myself at the very front of the boat, as if that would make it go faster.

The column of smoke was pushed higher and higher by the fire that the earth was constantly spitting out. At the top, it spread out in a sheet that darkened the sky towards the south. We were advancing in a greyish fog that thickened by the minute. Objects began to fall into the water around us. One of them pierced the sail, burning it. It was a rain of incandescent stones. Theodossis decided to turn back.

"These stones will damage the boat or hurt us. Besides, the wind is changing. It will push us towards Hattiarina and we will not be able to return."

Lightning crackled above us. To stop hearing this crash, I was squeezing my hands over my ears so hard I could break my skull. But the noise was everywhere. It made the whole boat, my guts, my bones vibrate. I, who laughed at those who secretly went to worship in the caves, began to pray. I begged the god Enki to save my family. I promised him to do everything he would ask of me, to give him everything I had. I offered him my life in exchange for theirs.

§

Theodossis's sister and their friends had returned to Ios. They had gathered our belongings on the covered terrace, along with some fruit, dried fish, and water. Exhausted, Theodossis fell asleep while I rekindled the fire to warm up some leftover vegetables for him. Everything was grey. The beach, rocks, and bushes were covered in ash, and a carpet of pumice stones floated on the sea. The sun was nothing more than a brown disk emitting a gloomy light. I tried to imagine what the people of Urukinea had done, but I couldn't focus. I had only trivial thoughts like regret for having botched my last investigation report or guilt for not having taken the time to repair Adikete's fresco. With an empty mind, I watched the waves sluggishly kneading a greyish mud.

The night was terrible. We had built a kind of tent with tamarisk branches to breathe as little dust as possible. Every time I began to fall asleep, an explosion woke me up with a start, trembling all over. Only the warmth of Theodossis's skin against mine kept me in touch with life. Without him, I would have died of anguish on this beach. The next day, through the veil of dust, the sun no longer warmed us. We shivered with cold and fatigue. At Hattiarina, the earth was still ceaselessly rumbling. The island had disappeared, wrapped in the twilight mist down to sea level. Beyond, it was pitch black. We prepared the boat like ghosts.

Seen from the sea, covered in ashes, Ios looked sinister. When we arrived at the port, everyone was waiting for us on the quay. As we docked, they tried to smile at us, but it was anguish that could be read in their eyes.

§

Ash was everywhere, in the streets, on the terraces, in the houses, in the cupboards, in the beds. With Anthea, Theodossis's mother, and Penelope, we spent our time dusting inside and sweeping in front of our house. Every day, we had to evacuate buckets and buckets of ashes. Everyone did the same. We had a garden at the bottom where we could pile ours, but in the village, people were forced to dump them in the street. Without respite, day and night, there was a continuous rumbling, interspersed with crackles and explosions. At night, even through the blankets stretched over the windows, lightning illuminated the rooms.

Tensions began to rise between the people. The altercations multiplied for increasingly futile pretexts. One day, I made a remark to our neighbour who was shaking his carpet above our terrace. He immediately flew into a mad rage, calling me all the names under the sun and insulting Theodossis' family. Penelope came to the rescue. There was no way to calm him down. On the contrary, his wife got involved in turn, accusing Penelope of sleeping with the whole village and saying that she was not surprised that they were harbouring a "black head". When she said that I would have done better to stay in Hattiarina and disappear with all the Hattianteans, I came down from the terrace to go and break her nose. If Theodossis and Panos had not returned at that moment, it would have ended badly. They went to the neighbour's house themselves. Mixed with Hattiarina's rumbles we heard shouts of voices and then the sound of furniture and dishes being knocked over. When they returned, they looked satisfied.

As the days went by, more and more serious events occurred. One night, we were awakened by the screams of a woman wandering the street, an unconscious child in her arms. For some time, her son had been feverish. He had difficulty breathing and was coughing constantly. Not hearing him anymore, she went to his room and found him lifeless. She wanted to go drown herself with him. Penelope and I spent the rest of the night with her, to bring her back to reason. The death of this child was added to the deaths of several elderly people, probably because of the dust that we breathed all day long and which poisoned the food and water.

The worst came soon after. The ash carried by the water accumulated in the walls of the wells, until they were completely clogged. By the tenth day, no well in the village was giving water. There was only one small spring left on a hill overlooking the harbour and another, more abundant, but located in the centre of the island, a four-hour walk away. In the tired state the people were in, it was impossible for them to go so far to get water. Panos then suggested using the donkeys to organise a caravan. After a few days they would get used to the journey and three or four people would be enough to watch over them. This idea made us realise another problem. We would need a lot of hay to feed the donkeys. However, since the explosion, we had been taking more care of the houses than the fields. This was a mistake. Instead of sweeping our terraces all day long, we should have cleaned the pastures. The next day, Theodossis arrived home brandishing a curious rake. He had spent the whole night at the port in his shed to make a tool halfway between a straw broom and a hay rake. We went straight away to try it out in the garden. It worked rather well. In two or three strokes of this "rake-broom", the grass reappeared.

Panos thought for a few moments then, suddenly, he said:

"We have to mobilise everyone to organise the donkey convoy and clean the fields. There is a council tomorrow. Asiraa, you will come with me and explain to them. I will warn the governor. I know he will agree."

A Hattiantean woman at the council of an Achaean village! It seemed difficult and, after the altercation with the neighbors, I didn't believe it at all. They would turn their backs before even starting to listen to me. But Panos insisted. He claimed that if it were him who spoke to them, they would invoke all sorts of inconveniences demonstrating that it was more prudent to do nothing. On the other hand, he affirmed that they would listen to me without daring to contradict me. I doubted it but I could not shirk.

The governor introduced me as the companion of Panos' son without further details. He justified my presence by my skills in city administration. After insisting on the fact that the situation was serious, Panos explained the problem of the wells. Then he handed me over to speak without giving them time to react. Adopting his tactic, I entered without preamble into the explanation of the solutions we were proposing for water and crops. I tried to hide my Hattiantean accent as best I could (even if they knew very well what was going on) and I pretended not to notice those who tried to speak. As soon as I had finished, after a short silence, Panos thanked me and asked me to leave the session to let the council continue its deliberations. Back home, he told me the rest.

"They are good people, but they have the big fault of preferring to talk rather than act. If I had suggested to them to clean the fields or to send the donkeys to fetch water, we would still be talking. You, I don't know how you do it, but when you talk, people listen to you and believe you. We just had to not give them time to react."

Panos took matters into his own hands. He requisitioned the most valiant donkeys and had them equipped to carry water. The caravan was set up immediately. He charged Theodossis with gathering volunteers to mass-produce broom rakes and he appointed a member of the council to organise the raking of the meadows. This mobilisation was finally well accepted by the people of the village who needed to be directed and to feel active against the disaster.

§

For three weeks the earth had been vomiting its entrails on Hattiarina. Three weeks without ever sleeping or eating well, breathing dust that got everywhere and dried out the mouth and throat, trying to solve problems that never stopped popping up one after the other and, for me, to dwell day and night, until dizziness, on the same unanswered questions about what could have happened to my mother, my brother, my cousins, my friends. I had the feeling that nature no longer wanted us. We continued to rake the fields, to carry the ashes, to tend the animals, to try to grow vegetables. We continued to live, but we no longer knew why.

Then, one morning, I woke up with the impression of having slept better than usual. The rumbling was less loud and, above all, there were no more explosions. I rushed to the terrace. The thick fog of ash that had completely enveloped Hattiarina had dissipated, revealing once again the column of smoke above the island. It was still riddled with lightning, but it was budding less and there was no more fire inside. Was the nightmare going to end? We didn't dare believe it.

The following days, the calm confirmed. In the morning, we had less dust to sweep and the sky, brighter, became blue again. It was still a pale blue, almost grey, but it was enough to give us hope. We could finally work without having to start all over again the next day and by resting at night. The village, like the sky, also regained its colours. One by one, the wells were put back into operation. Like Anthea who was soon to have a dozen chicks, everyone was busy rebuilding their resources. However, I could not rejoice in this return to life. Instead of fading, the question of what had become of all those I loved obsessed me and made me more and more anxious. Theodossis urged me to participate in the rebirth of his village, but the enthusiasm that reigned only accentuated my despair. Deep down, I was ashamed to be alive.

One day I was raking a new plot where Panos wanted to replant vegetables. The layer of ash was packed down and I was making no progress. I was keeping my mind occupied by trying to count how many raking strokes I had left to do when suddenly I had the impression that Adikete was right behind me. He was crying and calling for help. It sent shivers down my spine. The next night I couldn't sleep. Sitting on the bed, I still had the impression I could hear him crying. What if he had survived? Maybe I could feel his anguish. After all, there could be places where people had taken shelter. I woke Theodossis.

"Take me to Hattiarina. I want to know what happened."

Without turning around, he grumbled.

"You might regret it. Think carefully."

"I want to know."

§

We were about to pass the southern tip of Ios and yet we still did not see Hattiarina. Several times, seized with anxiety at the thought that it had been submerged, I almost asked Theodossis to turn back. We finally saw the outline of the island only after more than an hour of sailing. From Ios, we could not see it because it was too bright. Completely covered in ashes, it merged with the mist. When we arrived about ten stadiums from the coast, we still could not distinguish a single house or tree. The island emanated a heat that we felt from the boat. There was no longer any relief. Everything had been erased. Hattiarina had disappeared under dozens of cubits of ashes forming a single smooth yellowish surface. We didn't recognise anything any more. How could it be that our island, after having fed us so generously for a thousand years, suddenly wanted to destroy us?

We knew we had passed Aphaia when we saw the red cliff just beyond the port. Theodossis wanted to stop to eat and rest before returning. He landed at the foot of the cliff. I went in search of driftwood to cook the fish he had caught during the crossing. I found some right away. Lots of it. Pieces of wood, charred but that had visibly been painted in bright colours. I knew these colours well: they were those of Aphaia's boats. I sat down at the water's edge, contemplating these colourful planks scattered on the beach. It was almost looking nice. Theodossis came to sit next to me. Devastated, I could only snuggle against him.

§

To keep me from thinking, Theodossis gave me no respite. Although usually so taciturn, he was talking to me constantly. About everything, about nothing, without caring whether I was listening or not. He told me about his day of fishing, he gave me news of the hysterical neighbours or his mother's farmyard. Anthea, Penelope and even Panos got involved too. They always found excuses to absolutely need my help. These attentions comforted me, but the pain and despondency did not leave me. At night, horrible nightmares were waking me up, trembling with anxiety. I was so afraid of them that I no longer wanted to fall asleep. One night, I dreamed that I was struggling in the open sea in gigantic waves. Just as I was about to drown, I jumped out of bed, waking Theodossis with a start.

"You can't go on like this. You have to pull yourself together."

"I should never have left. I abandoned them. I hate myself."

"What are you saying? You didn't abandon anyone. You couldn't have known what was going to happen."

"So why did I want to leave just before?"

"It's just chance. You have nothing to do with it."

"And why am I the only one who was spared?"

"That's how it is. The rampages of our Earth are blind. They don't care about sparing this or that person. Stop looking for explanations where there are none."

"Do you remember? Several times, on the beach, I felt like the ground was shaking. Since you all told me you didn't feel anything, I didn't insist. Now I'm sure it was real. I should have believed it and returned to Hattiarina."

"And what would that have been for?"

"At least I would have died with them. First my father. Now my mother, my brother, my cousins, they have all disappeared. I have no one left. The neighbour was right. It would have been better if I had stayed there."

"Stop it! What happened to you is terrible but now, stop feeling sorry for yourself, it doesn't lead anywhere … And besides, not everyone has disappeared. I'm still there."

Getting aware of what I had said, I didn't dare turn around for fear of meeting his gaze. It was he who broke the interminable silence that followed.

"Until you know what happened to your family, you will continue to torture yourself with questions. If there were survivors, they certainly went to Kephti. It is a Hattiantean land and the wind carried them there. I will take you there. We will stay as long as it takes until you know what happened to your family and you are free of the demons that keep us apart."

Between the anxiety of being confronted with an unbearable reality and the hope of finding survivors, I no longer knew what I wanted.

"What's wrong? You don't want to go?"

I forced myself to stammer:

"Yes, yes. You're right. Take me."

§

KEPHTI

As soon as Ios merged with the horizon in the distance, I felt better. It was a selfish feeling, but there, despite the kindness of Theodossis' family, I was suffocating. Just the two of us with the sea and the sky, I could finally let my thoughts wander freely. A song my grandmother had taught me came back to my mind. As I hummed it, Theodossis asked me what it was.
"It is a very old song that dates back to before the founding of Urukinea. All the Hattianteans know it."
"What is it about?"
"It's about me. Listen."

Celebrate Isthar, the most august of Mothers,
Honored be the Sovereign of women, the greatest of all
She is joyful and clothed in love.
Full of seduction, femininity, voluptuousness
Joyful Isthar clothed in love,
Full of seduction, femininity, voluptuousness
Her lips are all honey her mouth is alive

At the sight of her, joy exults
She is majestic, her head covered with jewels
Splendid are her curves, her eyes, piercing and vigilant
She is the goddess to whom one can ask for advice.
The fate of all things she holds in her hands
From its contemplation joy is born,
Joy of life, glory, luck, success
She loves good understanding, mutual love, happiness,
She holds benevolence
The girl she calls has found a mother in her
She points her out in the crowd, she says her name
Who? Who can match her greatness?

"And this is a song about you?"
"Full of seduction, femininity and voluptuousness. Isn't that me?"
"There are many others."
"I thank you! And don't you think splendid are my curves?"
"Yes, and also that a conceited little person you are!"
"I'm kidding you! I was saying it's about me because of the end of the song, when it says, "The girl she calls has found a mother in herself, she points her out in the crowd, she says her name." It reminds me of what Mother Inanna told me."
He went back to his navigation, grumbling.

§

In order not to arrive at night, Theodossis decided to stop at Askania, a tiny islet lost in the open sea, about a third of the way to Kephti. We arrived there in the late afternoon. Much more ash had fallen on it than on Ios. The layer was so thick that it was nothing more than a uniform yellowish dome. It looked like a lump of butter floating on the water. This meant that the north wind had pushed the ash cloud towards Kephti. The state of this islet made me fear that it too might have been hit. Theodossis affirmed that at more than four hundred stadiums, it was much too far away.

Since the ash cloud had dissipated, the sun was turning brown in the early afternoon. As the sun set, the sky would take on unusual purplish-red colours, then a freezing cold set in quickly. That evening, wrapped up in our sheepskins, the world was reduced to the warmth and smell of Theodossis. I would have preferred to stay awake to enjoy it as much as possible, but with the small waves rocking the boat, I didn't last long.

The next day, because of the tailwind, it was almost too hot on the boat. We were able to talk, argue and laugh normally. We even tried to make love, but in the bottom of the boat, with the heat and the rolling, I had to stop halfway. At midday, Kephti appeared on the horizon. Obviously, despite the distance to Hattiarina, the ash cloud had reached it. We could see the houses, the trees and even vineyards in places, but the fields and the mountain were uniformly grey.

We had decided to disembark at Kamaljia, the great city on the northern coast. I knew its Matriarch. During my

internships, Mother Inanna had introduced me to her during one of her visits to Hattiarina. I thought she could help us. At the port, only one boat was docked. Its owner, repairing a sail, paid no attention to our arrival. Unfriendly, he deigned to explain to us that everyone was at sea all day because the fishing was almost no longer yielding anything. When Theodossis asked him where the harbour master's office was, he rolled his eyes and went back to his work. As we moved away to try and find someone more talkative, he shouted:
"You better not leave anything in your boat."
Theodossis bundled our clothes and I took the little water and food we had left. Realizing that nothing was working at the port any more, we set off straight for Kamaljia. The road had been cleared. On both sides, the ash bank was knee-high. In the fields, here and there, dark masses protruded from the grey layer. As we approached one of them, a flock of crows flew away, cawing. They were the rotting carcasses of cows.

Between the port and the city, the road crossed a village. The streets cluttered with ashes, it seemed to have been deserted by its inhabitants. Just after, at the entrance to Kamaljia, there were baths whose roof had collapsed into the basin. With each step, we realised a little more that Kephti was in an even worse state than Ios. As we climbed the main staircase, we heard a rumour coming from the Central Square. It seemed comforting at first, but when we came out onto the esplanade, we were shocked. Hundreds of people were sitting there, in groups, most around a fire. Kamaljia was invaded by refugees who had fled the countryside that had become uninhabitable.

Some had set up shelters with pieces of wood and canvas. The smoke made the air unbreathable. An oppressive calm reigned. Stunned, unable to enter this crowd, we sat down on a curb at the entrance to the square. Kephti was ravaged. If survivors of Hattiarina had made it this far, what had become of them in this chaos? I called out to a young woman who was distributing soup to ask her where the matriarchal premises were. She nodded to me in their direction.

Inside the building, it was very dark. The corridors were cluttered with objects that people had brought without realizing that they would be of no use to them. The acrid smell of torches burned the throat. In the gloom, one could make out families who had probably not found a place on the esplanade. The Matriarch's office was open. Mother Nanshe saw us.

"Who's there?"

"I am Asiraa of Urukinea, Mother."

She didn't answer.

"I was introduced to you by Mother Inanna during one of your visits to Hattiarina."

"Asiraa? But how is that possible?"

"I was not in Hattiarina at the time of the explosion."

"Give me a minute. You're going to explain it to me."

Mother Nanshe was the opposite of Mother Innana. Small, thin, carefully made up, she spoke nervously, which gave a false impression of aggressiveness. Her office was decorated with a large, very cheerful fresco depicting the harvest festival. When she noticed that I was avoiding looking at it, she confessed that it had the same effect on her. She had considered hiding it, but she had left it there to remind herself that it was up to her to bring back those happy times. I told her how I had escaped the catastrophe and, with great effort to control my emotion, the state in which we had seen Hattiarina.

"You were very lucky."

I refrained from telling her that I didn't know if it was a luck or a curse. She described to us what had happened to Kephti.

"Within a few hours, the ash cloud has darkened the sky. By the second day, at midday, it was darker than a full moon night. It was very distressing. The ash was falling in flakes covering everything. Lu-Dumuzi, our General Intendant, immediately took matters in hand. He had the warehouse openings covered to protect the reserves and he mobilised everyone to clear the roofs that were threatening to collapse. Then, he imposed strict rationing, in particular by prohibiting the use of cereals for making beer. The population responded well. What saved us was that we did not lack water. The main source that supplies Kamaljia comes from the depths of the mountain. It still flows abundantly and it is not corrupted."

"In the countryside, it was quite different. The wells quickly became unusable. Without food and water, helpless, the peasants came here to take refuge by the hundreds. Those who could not come down from the mountains are probably dead by now. We could not go and rescue them. There was too much to do here. Now we survive on reserves and fishing. What worries me is next winter. We managed to save some of the city's flocks, but apart from a few cows and a few donkeys that refugees brought, all the livestock in the countryside has died, poisoned by the ashes. The summer crops are lost and we don't know when we'll be able to put the fields back into cultivation. For now, we're living from day to day, but we're certainly going to face great difficulties."

I told her the reason for our coming to Kephti.

"No survivors' boat has arrived here. But since the explosion, we have been cut off from the world. There may have been some elsewhere."

The Intendant Lu-Dumuzi intervened.

"I heard that a fisherman saw a sail of Hattiarina off the coast of Chaminjia."

"Where is Chaminjia?" Theodossis asked.

"It is about a hundred stadiums from here, towards the east. But I advise you not to go there. The further east you go, the more ashes there are. The road must be impassable and it must be terrible over there. I can imagine what you feel, Asiraa, but I implore you: flee this hell, return to Ios."

"Can we go there by boat?" Theodossis insisted.

"Yes, it is possible, but it takes longer because there is a large cape to go around," confirmed the General Intendant.

§

On the way to the port, Theodossis thought aloud.

"There is still a chance that this boat existed. We will make a detour via Chaminjia before returning to Ios. It will add two or three days, but we will know how it stands."

Suddenly he swore in Achaean with words I did not know. Beside himself, he was looking around and shouting.

"Where is our boat? Someone stole our boat!"

"It's terrible. What are we going to do?"

"We'll wait for them. I'll show them how we treat thieves where we are from, you'll see."

A man approached.

"They won't come back. People from Kunisuu stole it. I live at the entrance to the port. I saw them arrive. Your boat is going to fish for Issessinak now."

"Issessinak?"

"The General Intendant of Kunisuu. He's the one who runs everything there. As for the Matriarch, no one sees her any more. Some even say she's dead."

"But a General Intendant cannot rule the city by himself."

"You are right, young girl... but these days, who could we complain to? Who has enough strength left to prevent Issessinak from doing what he wants?"

"How could this happen?"

"Because of her poor health, their Matriarch increasingly relied on her General Intendant. Everyone who went to Kunisuu said that the climate there was strange. They held extravagantly lavish festivities, and yet people always looked sad. In the countryside, the peasants complained that the city was always demanding more of their crops. After the catastrophe, things got worse. The city closed itself off. We don't know how they live inside any more. They say they force the women and children to work."

Theodossis insisted on ways to recover his boat. The man was adamant.

"They take everything that can be used for supplies, so a fishing boat, …! They'll repaint it and you'll never see it again."

Distraught, we returned to Kamaljia to spend the night. In the Central Square, we settled down near a fire around which three families were warming themselves. As I looked at the crowd, I noticed that very few people were moving and that nobody was entering or leaving the square. Nothing was happening any more. They were overwhelmed by the extent of the disaster.

We had only a little bread and a dried mackerel left. The hot oatmeal that was distributed to everyone was welcome. Unable to find a comfortable position to sleep, we spent the night discussing what we could do. There was no question of staying in this place. We decided to go to Chaminjia on foot. We could at least learn what this boat was about before trying to figure out how to get back to Ios. But we did not have enough food left to travel by road. Only the Matriarch could decide to give us some. We returned to see her.

"Mother Inanna had high hopes for you, Asiraa. In her memory, I want to help you. I have a she-ass whose foal died two days ago. You will take her. She will carry your load and she will give you milk. She is strong. You can ride on her if you are tired. You will be given oats for her and for you. Unfortunately, I cannot do more."

The Intendant suggested that we take a bow and arrows. According to him, there was still small game under the bushes and near the hedges. Mother Nanshe took me to see her donkey. Her name was Waspi. With her white muzzle and her eyes ringed with the same, one would have thought that she was wearing makeup. I fell in love with her immediately and it was probably mutual because she followed me without hesitation.

§

We left the next day at dawn. On the horizon, in the direction of Hattiarina, we could see the column of smoke. It was nothing more than a thin line that dispersed very high in the sky. Under our feet, the layer of ash was irregular. In places it was pasty, even sticky, while elsewhere a crust had formed that broke under our feet. Waspi was a good beast. To pass the time, I talked to her. I told her stories about life before in Urukinea, or else I explained to her what we were going to do once we arrived in Chaminjia. Theodossis found it ridiculous to talk to a donkey. I was sure she was happy that we were talking to her. She too must have found the time long. And she too must have been scared in this sinister landscape.

On the second day, we reached the highest part of our route. Because of the wind, the layer of ash there was thinner and very hard. The walk was less tiring than the day before. All around us, we could only see the uniformly grey fields on which stood out the skeletons of the leafless trees. I was walking, my mind lost in this lifeless landscape, when I saw, below, a very clear dark rectangle. Someone had cleaned a plot of land on which, wisely tied to its stake, a goat was grazing on sparse but green grass. It shared its small meadow with two chickens and a duck. The owner's house was a little further away, hidden in a grove of trees, also green. As soon as we approached, the peasant came towards us. Despite his beard, his long hair and his threadbare clothes, he didn't look like a destitute man. He stood straight, looking menacing, holding a metal-pronged pitchfork in both hands.

"Whoever you are, move on. There is nothing here that I want to share with you."

I assured him that we had everything we needed and that we expected nothing from him. He lowered his pitchfork.

"I come from Hattiarina. I escaped the disaster and we are looking for other survivors."

Contrary to what he said, he was dying to talk to someone. Returning to his old self, he suggested that we come and have a bowl of cider. Before the explosion, he was operating this farm with two workers. He had vines, apple trees and a herd of goats. From the first days, they had organised themselves to try to save at least part of the farm. They shook the branches of the trees to clean the leaves and they cleared plots with shovels. But every day, everything had to be redone. The workers had become discouraged and, like most of the other landsmen, they had left for Kamaljia. He refused to leave his land. He tirelessly cleaned the small meadow, "morning and evening so that the grass would not be smothered". He also set up a kitchen garden where a few vegetables were beginning to emerge, watered by a spring that was still flowing. Of all his animals, he had only been able to save the ones we had seen.

I asked him why he was so suspicious.

"Things have changed a lot in Kephti. You people in Hattiarina didn't realise it. I know it because one of my cousins worked in Aphaia. Here, for several years, evil has been spreading. It was because of the Intendant Issessinak. This scoundrel took advantage of the Matriarch's weakness to seize the city and impose his destructive power on it. He is a bastard with Egyptian blood in his veins. He is jealous of Kamaljia and Payto, the two other great cities of Kephti. Like the pharaoh, he has built ever larger, ever more pretentious buildings, which only serve to flatter his pride. It is said that his apartments are insanely luxurious."

"My daughter is a hairdresser. She works most often in Kamaljia, but she also goes to Kunisuu. She has seen things there get worse from month to month. Before the explosion of Hattiarina, the city had already become unbearable to live in. Issessinak's henchmen terrorised everyone. Woe to anyone who complained, or worse, who criticised the General Intendant. Those who took the risk disappeared for several days and when they returned, nothing could be gotten out of them."

"Does your daughter still go to Kunisuu?"

He stayed staring blankly for a few moments.

"The week before the disaster, she told me she wanted to quit her job and come back to the farm. She liked looking after animals and she knew how to make cheese. The day before the explosion, she went to work in Kamaljia. She was supposed to return three days later, but with the ashes falling and the darkness, she probably didn't want to take the road. When the weather cleared, she still didn't return. So I went to Kamaljia. The people she was going to told me she had come, but they didn't know what she had done afterwards. Kunisuu's militias abducted her, I'm sure of it. They're always roaming around Kamaljia, ransoming and stealing. And they abduct women."

"They abduct women! What for?"

"I don't know. What is certain is that, since the disaster, women have disappeared. My daughter is one of them. Believe me, be careful. They are lurking everywhere."

This story of abductions might have seemed improbable, but after the theft of our boat, we could wonder.

"I hope you find your family in Chaminjia, but I warn you: it's even worse there than here. You won't be able to stay."

From the beginning, he was manipulating a small clay object that intrigued me.

"This was her seal to enter Kunisuu. She didn't want to go there any more. Take it. If chance puts her on your path, you will show it to her and tell her that I am still alive and waiting for her. Her name is Ninissina, daughter of Lugal-Kahn."

I took the seal without being able to tell him that we intended to go back to Ios and that there was no chance that we would find his daughter. He hugged me for a long time.

"Thank you for stopping by my place. May your love protect you."

§

A little further on, Theodossis spotted a large clump of juniper trees below. Under these types of shrubs, the ground had remained bare. He hoped to be able to flush out rabbits or partridges that had come looking for food. Promising that we would finish with the oatmeal porridge with donkey's milk, he decided to set up our camp at the side of the road and left. Just in case, I started milking Waspi.

"That's a really nice beast you have there!"

A shiver of fear ran down my spine. Freeing myself from Waspi, I stumbled and found myself on the ground. Two men were looking at me, snickering. A tall bearded man and a short, fat one. They were both dressed the same way, with a vest, a skirt, a woollen cape, and sheepskin boots. Almost new, these clothes made them look like city clerks.

"Excuse me, I didn't mean to scare you. This milk looks delicious. We were wondering if you'd be willing to give us some."

While the bearded man was rummaging through our things, he was waddling toward me. His small eyes were sunken into the fat of his puffy face. He pulled a dagger from his belt. Still on the ground, trying to back away, my hand hit a large dead branch. I grabbed it and waved it in front of me to try to keep him at a distance.

"You know how to defend yourself. Good. I love it when they resist."

Before I could react, he lunged at me. He was blocking my arms with his knees, pressing his dagger to my throat. I screamed in pain. He slapped me brutally.

"Shut up or I'll slit your throat!"

Leaning forward, with his free hand, he tried to get his penis out. I didn't dare move any more, for fear that his knife would cut my throat. His sidekick left our pack.

"Wait. Hold her still, I'll make her wet."

He ripped off my skirt. I threw my legs around trying to kick him. He snickered.

"Block her legs, she's wiggling all the time."

The fat one stretched out on top of me, holding my arms and spreading my thighs with his knees. I was suffocating. The other one started to search my sex.

"Mmm, you like …"

There was a small dull noise. He removed his hand, stood up, gesticulating, and fell forward, straight. The little fat man only had time to start getting up. I saw the tip of the arrow come out of his chest. He opened his mouth, stayed like that for a few moments before collapsing on top of me, digging the tip of the arrow into my shoulder. With a kick, Theodossis rolled him aside. The bearded man was dead. In his death throes, the little fat one was gasping. Theodossis finished him off by slitting his throat, then he pushed the two corpses to the side of the road and covered them with ashes.

Sitting on a rock, shaking uncontrollably, I sobbed trying to explain what had happened. Theodossis rubbed my back to try to stop me from shaking. When I could think again, I had only one idea: to wash myself. We didn't have much water, but the repugnant traces had to be rubbed out. I think I could have scrubbed with a pumice stone. Despite the late hour, I mounted Waspi and we set off again. I was in pain everywhere. My arms were covered in bruises and my shoulder wound was burning. I thought back to Ninissina, the farmer's daughter. The poor woman had probably had to deal with brutes of this kind.

We walked all night, until we reached the pass overlooking Chaminjia bay. On the other side of the mountain, the layer of ash was again very thick. We sank in mid-calf. Fortunately, I had Waspi to carry me. I would never have had the strength to continue. On her back, half unconscious, everything kept coming back to me: the sight of the man advancing towards me, the anguish of being trapped under his weight and the horrible sensation of the fingers violating me.

§

The road led first to the port of Chaminjia. As in Kamaljia, it was deserted. We were each looking for someone to give us information when Theodossis called me. He had discovered an abandoned boat at the bottom of the port. The mast broken, filled with ashes covering what must have been the sails, a breach open on one side, it was in pitiful condition. The prow was submerged almost to the gunwale but we could still clearly see the decorations of Hattiarina. I didn't dare believe it.

"Don't get carried away", Theodossis said. "It looks very bad. It might have been here before the explosion."

I, on the contrary, was convinced that this boat had arrived here after the catastrophe. The damage corresponded to the rain of stones that we ourselves had suffered. It could have saved dozens of people. In this case, they must still be in the city of Chaminjia which was a few stadiums from the port.

§

As Mother Nanshe and Lugal-Kahn had told us, on this side of Kephti the layer of ashes was more than a cubit thick. The trees had lost their leaves and, in the fields, carcasses of dead animals lay everywhere. No meadows had been cleared. In the city itself, only the long main street was more or less clear. In the alleys, the ashes were barely packed in the middle by the passage of people. When we reached the Central Square, we finally came across a woman. She was bending under the weight of two buckets hanging from a yoke on her shoulders. I asked her where to go to see the Matriarch. She had died two weeks before and the new one was in Kamaljia to introduce herself to Mother Nanshe. She suggested that we go see the Intendant, showing us the direction of his office. In her hurry to continue on her way, she forgot us. The Intendant was not there either. There was only one city worker busy sweeping up the ashes. He said that if there were people from Hattiarina, they would certainly be in the refugee camp below the city.

In a deep valley, hundreds of families who had fled the countryside were crammed into an inextricable tangle of shacks. Only a few children were playing in the narrow alleys. I asked one of them to take us to his parents. He led us to a hut made of tamarisk branches on the walls and skins on top. Inside, I was only just able to stand. Theodossis, as for him, was forced to remain bent over. The only light was the glow of the fire heating a pot whose smell made me retch. I could not even see how many people there were in this small place. Without hesitation, the woman who was tending the pot confirmed to us that there were indeed people from Hattiarina gathered at the other end of the valley.

I had come hoping to hear this, but I did not know it would be such a shock. I had to sit down. The fear of facing the worst outweighed the joy of learning that there were survivors. The thought of running away crossed my mind. The woman took me in her arms. She whispered to me:

"You've been courageous to come this far. Go all the way."

We were wandering through the alleys of the neighbourhood she had told us about, when a little girl who came up behind us pulled me by the sleeve. Seeing my face, she ran away shouting, "Mummy, Mummy, it's Asiraa, she's here, I saw her." She rushed into a hut and came out again immediately, followed by her parents. A crowd quickly formed around us. People besieged us with questions. A man asked them to move aside and leave us so he could talk to me alone. I recognised Sin-Andul and his wife, Lu-Ninurta, friends of my uncle who sometimes came to the house.

"It's a great joy to see you again, Asiraa... Your mother told us that you had gone to Ios...You must have been terribly anguished when you saw what was happening to our island..."

From his look, from the tone of his voice, I understood.

"You need to know... Those who survived are very few."

Seeing my distress, he hurried to continue.

"The day after you left, the earth began to shake again. Not as hard as the first time, but constantly. The ground was rumbling and shaking day and night. On the third day, the water in the inland sea became so hot that it was steaming. In the evening, an island appeared in the middle. It was a black mass of slimy rocks that slowly slid toward the cliffs of Hattiarina. The next day it already occupied half of the inland sea and it continued to grow. On the fifth day, the inland sea had completely disappeared. From the top of the cliff, the heat was unbearable and the dome of rock continued to rise. Mother Inanna and the General Intendant then decided to evacuate the island. The entire population gathered at Aphaia. At dawn on the seventh day, the embarkation had begun when there was a huge explosion. With a terrifying crash, the dome started spitting fire, throwing incandescent rocks hundreds of cubits high. People rushed. They got into the boats in too many numbers, carrying far too many objects. Out at sea, the first boats capsized and sank. The following boats left with fewer loads but still did not have enough room to use the oars. With only their sails, they were very slow. I was on one of them with my wife and my two sons. Your mother and Adikete followed on another boat. Then there was a series of explosions of unimaginable violence, throwing into the air rocks that were falling back on us. Some were the size of sheep. One of them smashed the boat where your mother and brother were. We could do nothing. They were more than two stadiums behind us, and, loaded as we were, it was impossible to turn back."

Until there, I had still hoped to learn that no one knew what had become of them. That would have allowed me to imagine what I wanted. He had just deprived me of this last resort. Seeing my tears flow, he interrupted his story.

"Go on, I said, I want to know what happened to the others."

"Then the explosions subsided. We were moving south, towards Kephti. Behind us, five or six stadiums away, we could see the line of ships leaving the port. Suddenly, with a dull roar, a huge grey cloud formed on top of the cliff, above Urukinea. It swept down the slope, engulfing the city and the port. Then it continued out to sea. What we saw at that time was dreadful. When the cloud was reaching the ships, they burst into flames like straws. Before they disappeared, we could see the people jumping into the water, transformed into living torches. We could hear the screams of terror of those who were seeing the cloud coming towards them. When …"

With trembling lips, he stammered:

"They all died, Asiraa… All of them."

Lost in his visions of terror, he could not say anything more. Lu-Ninurta encouraged him to continue.

"Only five boats arrived at Kephti. Our mast had been damaged. It threatened to break at any moment, so we took the shortest route by coming here. The other four went to Dikta, on the east coast. They wanted to get as far away from Hattiarina as possible to escape the rain of ash, but there it was even worse than here. It had fallen in large flakes and, in some places, the layer was already more than a cubit thick. One boat returned here. The others continued south with some of the inhabitants of Dikta."

"How many people were on those boats?" Theodossis asked.

"In all, about two hundred. Here, with those who returned from Dikta, there were eighty of us."

The rock smashing the boat, Adikete struggling not to drown, the burning cloud rolling over the sea, the people screaming in terror… I could no longer manage to listen to what they were saying. After a night spent on Waspi's back without sleeping, completely exhausted, overwhelmed by my emotions, I fainted.

§

I did not understand what I was seeing. I found myself in a dark and nauseating hovel. Theodossis was near me.

"Where am I?"

"Sin-Andul offered me this hut vacated following a death."

"How long did I sleep?"

"Almost two days. How do you feel?"

Rested, I felt a little better, despite the terrible images that were already coming back to me.

"It was good to sleep. What are we going to do now?"

"I have started looking to see if I could repair the damaged boat to return to Ios."

"Yes, let's go back. Let's get out of here. Anyway, we won't learn anything more."

He took me to see the boat. He had removed the sails and debris that covered the deck, making the damage even more apparent. The task seemed insurmountable.

"You think you can get through this?"

"You can always repair a boat if you have the necessary equipment. But it's not the case. I'm afraid it will take a lot of time."

We both needed to believe that we could escape this hell. Theodossis went in search of tools and materials, while I took care of preparing our departure. For everyone, finding water, food and heating was a constant concern. I also had to worry about saving enough to cover the journey. Thanks to these tasks that left me no respite, I thought less about Sin-Andul's story. However, a bitter feeling was still tormenting me. When our father died, I had promised Adikete that I would never abandon him. When I left for Kephti, I reiterated this promise. Now, certain that his last thought had been of my betrayal, I was haunted by the thought that I would never again be able to ask his forgiveness..

§

In the city, far from improving, the situation was getting worse by the day. A first attempt to dig a new well was a failure. The men had worked hard to go under the rock, in vain. Already difficult, water rationing had to be reinforced so as not to compromise the irrigation of the few cleared plots. Those who still could worked in the fields or went to sea, but with meagre results. The reserves were running out. One night, I heard noises around our hut. Theodossis went out to see. He arrived just in time to put to flight two men who had come to steal Waspi, no doubt to eat her. We were slowly weakening and many people were falling ill. I myself, from breathing dust and fumes all day, ended up bedridden with a fever and endless coughing fits. Thanks to the potions prepared by Lu-Ninurta, I recovered, but for many others, this was not the case. The deaths were increasing in number.
Beyond these material difficulties, the fate of the survivors of Hattiarina worried me. Theodossis and I were going to return to Ios, but they seemed condemned just to swell the ranks of a population in distress. Was I still going to be the only one who could extricate myself from the trap? When I tried to talk to Theodossis about it, he rebuffed me without restraint. He was working from morning to night on the repair of the boat and, the more time passed, the more irascible he became. I

had never known him in this mood. One evening he returned from his worksite, his expression defeated.

"What's wrong? What happened?"

"I lack everything: tools, wood, ropes, bitumen, everything. And as if that were not enough, last night I forgot to bring in some planks before closing the hold. This morning, of course, they were gone. I don't even blame the thieves. It's my fault. I should have just put my planks away."

"That doesn't excuse thieves."

"Sin-Andul is convinced that the boat is beyond repair. I am beginning to wonder if he is right. I do not know when we will be able to leave again."

I had always seen him display unwavering tenacity. For the first time, he seemed discouraged.

"Take your time. I'm sure you'll get there."

"If you are sure…"

§

I often stayed at the camp to entertain the children. One day, while I was playing with them in the Central Square, I saw three men arrive, among whom I recognised a student from the school of architecture. They were part of the group that had continued south after Dikta, continuing along the coast until reaching Payto. This region of Kephti had been very little affected by the ashes. The harvests had not been good because of the cold and the lack of sun, but neither the vegetation nor the animals had really suffered. A few stadiums from the city, there was a ruined village, abandoned. They were coming to offer us to join the survivors of Hattiarina who intended to ask from Mother Ninkilim, the Matriarch of Payto, permission to settle there. The description they gave us of an intact city, surrounded by meadows and cultivated fields, seemed unreal to us. As they spoke, Theodossis and I looked at each other, realizing that we were thinking the same thing: we had to stop persisting in repairing the broken ship and leave for Payto as soon as possible. If there was a way back to Ios somewhere in Kephti, that was where we would have the best chance of finding it.

The next day, Sin-Andul gathered all the survivors to explain the plan to settle in the abandoned village. Of course, they were enthusiastic about the idea of leaving Chaminjia for a region spared by the ashes. On the other hand, they were worried about the journey. The weakest or those who had charge of elderly people wanted to go by sea. The others argued over the best route to take, the northern one via Kamaljia and Kunisuu or the central one, crossing the mountains to the southern coast. I spoke.

"With only one boat, we won't all be able to leave all together by sea. The worst thing would be to separate. We have to leave by road."

The architecture school student continued.

"The winds are unfavourable all the way. From here, to go to Payto by sea, it takes two to three weeks, without any possibility of resupply. When we did it, we had brought enough water and we could still fish. Today and in the state of exhaustion you are in, it is no longer possible. Asiraa is right, you must leave by road."

I added:

"Whether by sea or by road, the journey will be made in suffering, cold and hunger. Let us choose a road and set off together. This is how we will overcome these ordeals and Hattiarina will live again."

There were some murmurs and then the debate resumed, but only on the road to take. The details given on the state of the road to the centre by those who had come from Payto got the better of the last hesitant people. It was decided to leave by the northern road. A week later, our caravan of disparate carts pulled by animals or by hand set off on the road to Kamaljia with a view to reaching Payto.

§

ISSESSINAK

Since our passage two months before, the ash had packed down. It took us only two days to reach Kamaljia, our first resupply stop. The refugees had continued to flow there, creating a new camp outside the city. Mother Nanshe told us that this exodus was accentuated by the harassment that the Kunisuu attendants were exerting on the peasants. They were becoming more and more threatening to force them to deliver their reserves to the city, and even their production for those who had started to cultivate again. Inside the city, things were not much better. The same diseases as in Chaminjia were raging. More than a hundred people had died and the number of sick people continued to increase. To take care of them as best they could, they had grouped them in unused sheds.

Due to the increasing influx of refugees, the Matriarch was unable to provide us with as much food as we would have liked. After a night's rest at the edge of the camp, we set off again at dawn towards the port of Kukkitiani, a day's walk away. We expected to find something there to complete our supplies.

During the trip, Theodossis was thinking about our future house. He wanted us to build one like the model I had made in Ios, on the beach. For me, building a new house would take too long. After what we had been through, I no longer had the courage to wait months to move in. I pretended to no longer remember the plans I had made. He then rummaged through our pack and took out the clay model. He had taken it without telling me when we had left the beach, carefully keeping the broken pieces and, of course, the figurines of us and our children. Defeated, I affirmed that, on second thought, we could live for a while with his parents while the work was being carried out.

Halfway before Kukkitiani, the road was running along the sea, overlooking it by a hundred cubits. The bay of Kunisuu with the island of Djia just opposite offered a magnificent spectacle. Theodossis and I were looking for names for our first child when people started shouting.

"Look! It takes up again."

A column of dazzling white was rising above the horizon, in the direction of Hattiarina. We all stopped, stunned. Nature had not finished with our island. Suddenly, across the entire width of the bay, I saw a huge gust of wind coming towards us at a dizzying speed. Behind it, the water was perfectly smooth. When it reached the shore, there was a huge detonation. It was not like the first time. There was no further explosion and we saw no fire in the column of smoke, which remained white.

In a few hours, increasingly dark clouds covered the sky and a torrential rain began to fall. We resumed our march to seek shelter as quickly as possible at Kukkitiani, but when we arrived there, we found the little port completely devastated. Everything was covered in mud, debris and corpses, animals and humans pell-mell. Most of the houses were destroyed. The boats were scattered in the countryside, some more than a stadium from the shore. Haggard survivors wandered in this desolation, soaked, covered in mud. One of them told us that about half an hour after the detonation, the port had emptied of water in a few minutes, up to a stadium or two from the shore. A short time later, the water had returned, but rising higher than the houses, carrying everything away into the plain: boats, carts, men, animals, everything. Then the water had receded, tearing up and destroying what was still standing. He had had time to climb into a tamarisk tree that had resisted the flood. Now he was desperately searching for his wife and his son. From where we were, we had seen nothing of this disaster.

We were all shivering with cold and fatigue. The road was impassable and we were not equipped to walk in the rain. The caravan could not set off again in this deluge. We set up camp on a hill overlooking the port. All afternoon, I was occupied by a fixed idea: to dry our clothes. I wanted to be stronger than the elements, but, with an anaemic fire and with the humidity that was everywhere, it was impossible. This insignificant failure infuriated me. I wanted this unleashing of blind forces that were relentlessly attacking us to stop.

Blocked by the rain, having been unable to resupply in Kukkitiani, the food problem was becoming critical. After Kamaljia, in order to avoid the militia of Kunisuu, we had planned to stop at Vatypetawa, located more than two days' walk from our camp. We had no choice but to go and ask for help in Kunisuu, only about thirty stadiums away. When it came to choosing who would go, Theodossis and I immediately volunteered. With what we had heard about this city, we wanted to see what it was like. We left early in the afternoon.

§

A few hundred cubits from the entrance to the city we were surprised to find the road blocked. A man wearing a bronze helmet and with a sword on his belt came out of a small building. I had never seen this in Hattiantean country. The principle, and the pride of the Great Federation was on the contrary the openness of all cities and the absence of men-at-arms. I claimed to be the new Matriarch of the survivors of Hattiarina, coming to ask for assistance from the Matriarch of Kunisuu. The guard looked me up and down then, suspicious, he called a colleague who had remained in the sentry box. Disturbed by the title of Matriarch, they hesitated on what to do. In doubt, the second guard signalled us to follow him.

The vast suburb surrounding the city of Kunisuu was surprisingly free of any trace of ashes. Even though the rain had been washing the ground for two days, there should have been piles in the squares or on street corners. Everything had been cleaned. The Central Square, also perfectly clean, was deserted. It was surrounded by buildings painted in garish colours. Inside, the profusion of decorations was surprising. In Urukinea or Kamaljia, in the administrative offices of the city, the walls were plain, with at most a few geometric patterns highlighting the door and window surrounds. There, everything was covered in ornaments in the same bad taste as on the outside. Examining the patterns in the room where we were waiting, I noticed a crack in the wall, curiously integrated into the design. By signs, I made Theodossis understand that we were probably being listened to on the other side of the wall. After a long wait, an attendant came to announce that General Intendant Issessinak was going to receive us and that in the meantime, he was going to show us around the Central House and the stores of Kunisuu so that we could see how well the city had come out of the disaster. Although I protested that I had not come to see the Intendant or to visit any buildings, we were forced to follow him.

According to our guide, the General Intendant had taken matters in hand and the population had rallied behind him to gather up reserves and repair the collective facilities. Theodossis was furious. He urged him to shorten his explanations, pointing out that everything he was showing us existed in any Hattiantean city. I signalled him to calm down, when, suddenly changing his attitude, he asked to visit a building we had just passed. Disturbed, the man stammered out confused explanations about a warehouse under renovation, inaccessible for security reasons. Nervous, he cut the tour short and took us back to the waiting room.

Two hours later, Issessinak finally arrived. Slender in stature, made up and coiffed in the Hattiantean style far from Egyptian fashion, he was not unfriendly. Only his blue tunic decorated with embroidery with golden yellow patterns was in the same bad taste as the decorations of the buildings. Friendly, he apologised for having kept us waiting, explaining that he had had to go and find out about the consequences of the floods on the coast. He confirmed that he had understood the purpose of my visit, but that being ill, the Matriarch would not be able to receive us until the next day. He suggested that we have dinner and spend the night in Kunisuu. We had not planned this, but we wanted to know more about the strange climate that reigned in the city. We accepted the invitation.

We were taken to a comfortable room where I was surprised to find a hot bath prepared for me. It was an unheard-of luxury. Why did Issessinak treat us so well? I led Theodossis out onto the covered terrace of the room to talk about it, all the more confidently as the sound of the rain drowned out our voices. I asked him why he had wanted to visit the closed warehouse.

"As I passed by, I heard people inside whispering. When I stopped, they fell silent. Approaching the door to listen, I smelled the typical odour of melted metal. Contrary to what he claimed, this is not a depot under construction. It is an active workshop that they want to hide from us."

§

Supper was served in a room decorated with sporting scenes: bull-jumping, fistfights, and spear-throwing. Their elegance suggested that they predated Issessinak's arrival as General Intendant. A multitude of Egyptian servants busied themselves around the table, all dressed alike in loincloths and short embroidered jackets. Issessinak excused Mother Nunbarshe and then introduced us to the other guests. He never made clear their status, except for one haughty-looking man whom he introduced by the surprising title of spiritual guide to the Matriarch.

In this type of reception, the Matriarch sat at the head of the table with the guest on her right. The Intendant's seat was in the middle of the table, on the left side. On the pretext that he would be too far from me, Issessinak sat in the Matriarch's place, which was very shocking. Theodossis, placed between two young women who devoured him with their eyes, was studying the guests attentively without paying the slightest attention to his neighbours.

The dishes that were served to us were like the entire reception, sumptuous but indecent in view of the deprivations suffered by the populations, including certainly that of Kunisuu. Issessinak did not give me a moment's respite. He first praised his actions at the time of the catastrophe. According to him, thanks to Mother Nunbarshe who had had the intelligence to delegate all powers to him right away, he had been able to act quickly and efficiently so that the population of Kunisuu had suffered little. When I expressed my surprise at the presence of armed guards at the entrance to the city, he justified this measure by the existence of looters coming from the countryside. As I insisted, asking him where the weapons came from, he replied that they were parade weapons that had always been in Kunisuu. I had clearly seen the sword of the guard who had stopped us when we arrived. It had a wooden handle and a rudimentary blade that had nothing to do with the swords decorated with gold and stones that were used for parades. He continued.

"Kephti is in a catastrophic state. The eastern part of the island has become uninhabitable. Dikta is already almost abandoned and you have been able to see the state Chaminjia is in. As for Kamaljia, it will not be able to support the thousands of refugees it has welcomed for long, especially since, as I learned this morning, it too was hit by devastating waves. Only three cities can get by: Kunisuu, Opsjia and Payto. We should join forces to regain the upper hand and save the Hattiantean people. I have already spoken to the Matriarch of Opsjia about it. She does not reject the idea of closer cooperation between our cities. On the other hand, the Matriarch of Payto does not want to hear about it. She is a very tough woman. I would like you to speak to her to convince her to receive me."

There we were. All this pageantry was just a way of buying our diligence with Mother Ninkilim. It displeased me to no end, though, unfortunately, he was not wrong about the state of Kephti. The idea of combining the efforts of the still valiant cities was worth considering. He concluded by assuring me that Mother Nunbarshe would be able to give us the supplies we needed to get to Payto.

Meanwhile, with the wine helping, Theodossis had abandoned his observations of the guests to take a closer interest in his neighbours. His Achaean accent made them cluck like turkeys and they swooned with admiration at the tale of his maritime exploits. All this was beginning to exasperate me. Pretending that it was an exhausting day, I asked Issessinak not to wait too long to finish the banquet. When he got up to ask his guests to kindly let us go, Theodossis gave me a furious look that I pretended not to understand. Once we returned to our room, after a spat about the two turkeys, we made love as we had not done for a long time: on a bed and making all the noise we wanted.

The next morning, the interview with the Matriarch took place as planned. Mother Nunbarshe entered, accompanied by a handmaiden. She was walking with difficulty and, to sit down, she needed the help of the General Intendant and her handmaiden. Her hand trembled and her head was moving incessantly from right to left. She stared at me for a long time with an expressionless look, then she said:

"How happy the people of Hattiarina must be to have such a young and pretty Matriarch. Those of Kunisuu are less fortunate. See what state I am in. Fortunately, my good Issessinak is here."

He was standing next to her. She took his hand and gave him an affectionate smile.

"Asiraa is leading the survivors of Hattiarina to Payto, Mother. She asks if we can give them some supplies."

"You have a lot of courage, Asiraa. Of course we will help you. You didn't need to ask me, Issessinak."

"In the current circumstances, I did not want to decide without talking to you, Mother."

"You know I trust you."

"I try to be worthy of it, Mother."

Surprised by these exchanges, I insisted that I be left alone with the Matriarch for a few moments. The General Intendant tried to protest, but Mother Nunbarshe motioned for him to accept.

"Just a minute, Mother. This interview is tiring you, you need to rest."

He left the room with the handmaiden. I asked Theodossis to follow them.

"Come closer, Asiraa, so I can see you better."

I knelt down to be at her height.

"Give me your hand."

She took my hand between hers. I could feel the terrible tremors that she tried to control by leaning on her knee.

"Thank you for coming to see me."

She was holding my hand, squeezing it too tightly.

"I am sad to see you so ill, Mother."

"Alas! This disease has been eating away at me slowly for three years. What misfortunes! How could we not see that the gods Enki and Utu are punishing us? Our immoral behavior has disappointed them. Their anger has fallen upon us. Fortunately, Intendant Issessinak has been able to take care of me as well as the city. He cares a lot about my health and he spares me a lot of fatigue."

I never thought I would hear a Matriarch, even weakened by illness, invoke the old superstitions that the Hattianteans had long since rejected.

"I see that he is very considerate with regard of you, Mother. But it seems to me that he is very alone in running the city. Have you thought about your succession?"

"Don't worry. He's taking care of it. He has already found several young women that he's going to introduce me to."

The General Intendant returned to end the interview. After the handmaiden had taken Mother Nunbarshe away, we agreed on the organisation of the provision of food. He did not fail to remind me of my diplomatic mission to the Matriarch of Payto. I promised to tell her about his plans for an alliance, without specifying whether I would support them or not, then, hypocritically, I congratulated him on having managed the city's problems while assuming the Matriarch's illness.

On the way back, we talked about this strange visit. Because of the swords of the guards and the smell of foundry, Theodossis was convinced that the closed room was a weapons factory. For me, the most disturbing thing was the relationship between Issessinak and Mother Nunbarshe. First, she showed him an abnormal affection and then, when the Matriarch was ill, it was the role of her handmaiden to be at her side, certainly not that of the General Intendant. As for Issessinak, he had a personality difficult to understand. One could not reproach him for his actions or his vision of the situation. However, during our entire visit, I had not ceased to feel uneasy.

§

During our absence, some inhabitants of the port who had lost everything had joined our caravan, which now numbered more than two hundred people. The main question that agitated the group was the best time to leave for Payto. On returning from the city, we had noticed that the road was very slippery, clogged with scree and even, in places, cut by torrents of mud. It seemed very risky to set off with the caravan there. Those in favor of leaving immediately argued that, not knowing how long they would have to wait, they risked leaving still in the rain and with depleted reserves. Finally, considering the few supplies that they had been able to recover in the ruins of the port, it was decided to wait a few days. The next day, a team went to Kunisuu. Issessinak kept his word and they returned with a cart loaded with provisions, while confirming the difficulties there were in traveling on the road.

Theodossis decided to go hunting, "to limit the consumption of reserves" he had said. In fact, obsessed with what he called the secret workshop, he was studying the functioning of the guard posts to prepare his return to Kunisuu. After two days of observations, he established his plan. At the northern corner of the city, a small post was manned by a single guard. Very few people passed through and the guard never set foot outside because of the rain. Theodossis wanted to enter through there and then wait for night to return to the workshop. I tried to dissuade him, of course, but without much conviction. I too wanted to know what Issessinak was up to.

Finding him Hattiantean clothes was not difficult. Making him a Hattiantean head was much harder. First, I had to hide his hair. I borrowed a young woman's wraparound bonnet to completely cover his typically Achaean curls. It was a very feminine model. To compensate, I made him up in an exaggeratedly masculine way. It suited him very well. When I suggested that I cut some locks of my hair to fix under his bonnet and make them stick out, I felt that I should not insist. Thus decked out, he left early in the afternoon, assuring me that he would be back the next morning.

After a night of insomnia and worry, the day dawned with a less dark sky and less heavy rain. This helped me to regain control a little. I managed to convince myself to trust him and to stop imagining the worst. When night fell, he still had not returned. Forcing myself to believe that he had preferred to wait until nightfall to leave Kunisuu, I waited until dawn, putting off the moment of admitting the obvious hour by hour. Finally, suddenly realizing that I had waited too long, I rushed to ask Sin-Andul for help. Unfortunately, his mind was on something else. Seeing the weather improving, he had decided to break camp and was mobilizing everyone to leave as quickly as possible. He apologised profusely, while insisting on Theodossis's recklessness in embarking on this expedition, alone and without warning anyone. I had no choice but to go myself. I only asked him to take Waspi and our burden so that we could find them when we caught up with the caravan on the road to Payto.

I was thinking about how to enter Kunisuu without being noticed. The solution came to me when, while packing our things, I found the seal of Ninissina, the daughter of the peasant we met on the road to Chaminjia. By posing as her, I could claim to come to work. It was a rough plan, but I had to be content with it.

§

The guard wasn't the same as the first time. He was slumped on a chair at the entrance to his sentry box, sheltered from the rain.

"I don't know you. Who are you?"

"Ninissina, daughter of Lugal-Kahn. I am a hairdresser."

He took the seal I handed him. After getting up, looking like he had made the effort of the day, he dragged himself inside, sighing. After a long moment, he reappeared.

"I can't find any imprint of your seal. You say you're a hairdresser?"

I remembered the name of a woman who was at dinner with Issessinak.

"Yes. I'm here to do Lu-Kuwanna's hair."

This name seemed to mean something to him.

"And why don't I have the imprint of your seal?"

"I don't know. I've been sick. I haven't been here for a long time. Maybe it got lost."

"Come in!"

With excruciating slowness, he pulled out a papyrus, sat down at a tiny table, and began to record me.

"Your name is…?"

"Ninissina."

As he was laboriously writing "Ninassina," I pointed out his mistake. He replied that he didn't care, but in the next room another guard reacted. He appeared in the door.

"You can read?"

I hadn't thought it was surprising that a hairdresser could read.

"When I was sick, I was bored, so I taught myself."

"And you can count, too?"

"Yes."

"Follow me!"

Without a word, he took me into the city and led me straight to a scribe's office.

"I heard you're looking for people who can count. This girl says she can."

He left immediately. The scribe handed me a clay tablet and a stylus.

"Write 12 plus 5 and write the result."

I complied.

"We're short of accountants here. The day the waves hit the shores, several of them were at the port to record the arrivals. They're all dead. I need someone at the South warehouses. You'll work there."

He rang a bell. A guard entered.

"Take her to the women's dormitory and hand her over to the chief."

Then, addressing me:

"Come back here tomorrow morning at the seventh hour."

I protested, reminding him that I had to do my client's hair.

He told me he would take care of it. I refrained from reacting.

§

The chief of the women's dormitory did not speak, she barked. After showing me my closet, she led me into the dormitory. Poorly lit by a few oil lamps, I could make out two rows of about fifteen beds separated by a small bedside table. There were no windows. She showed me my bed and ordered me to wait for the other girls to come back so that I could go with them to eat in the refectory. Sitting at the end of my straw mattress, I examined this sordid room that smelled of mould, sweat and urine. Issessinak had shown incredible duplicity. He had received us with great pomp while a few cubits away, women were treated like cattle. It was worse than anything that was being said outside.

At the eighteenth hour, the girls came back in. They didn't even notice me. They were whispering among themselves but none of them spoke to me. I tried to question my neighbour, in vain. Exasperated, I got up and shouted to everyone that I didn't understand what was going on and that I would have liked at least one of them to talk to me. The chief immediately came in:

"Who is yelling like that?"

She was holding a knotted whip that she was tapping nervously with her other hand. I was standing in the middle of the central aisle.

"Ah! The new one. It's you. Wait, I'll teach you how it works here when someone disturbs me."

She grabbed me by the shoulder, digging her fingers into the muscle and pressing down to make me kneel. The pain was so great that I could not resist. Holding me by the hair, she beat me with seven lashes with all her might. She left, barking:

"Understood, now?"

This episode had at least the merit of getting me noticed. During the meal, a girl came to sit down next to me to talk with me. She was from the countryside, somewhere between the port and the city. She was fifteen when they had come to get her in the field where she kept goats. Now she was working in a weaving workshop. Judging by the patterns on the fabrics, she thought they were destined for Egypt. When the ash rain had come, they had been forced to work day and night cleaning the streets, terraces and roofs. Two girls had died of exhaustion. She had been in Kunisuu for over a year, which confirmed that Issessinak was already raging before the Hattiarina disaster. I asked her about the existence of prisoners. She showed me, at another table, a girl who carried meals every evening to a guard, in the basement. She was speaking of a dungeon where several men were locked up. To find out more, I would have to wait until the next evening.

The following day I had to take inventory in a fabric warehouse. The scribe threatened me with lashes if I had not finished my task by the end of the day. After the beatings from the chief, I did my best to do so despite all the worries that assailed my mind. At dinner, I rushed to the girl who brought meals to the prison. Her name was Nin-Gula. She was a strong woman with an impressive chest and who did not mince her words. She had experienced the city's downward slide. At first, despite her authoritarian nature, Mother Nunbarshe was rather appreciated. Then, she had revealed herself to be more and more rigid, reproaching her subjects for being materialistic and immoral. When her illness had started, Issessinak had appeared next to her with the title of personal physician of the Matriarch. Shortly after, she had revoked her General Intendant to put Issessinak in his place. Together, they had reinstated the cult of Enki and Utu, the gods that our ancestors venerated. Then, an administrative building had been transformed into a temple where ceremonies were held. I was stunned. This measure openly violated the charter of the Great Federation which, as Queen Nanaya had wanted, banned all forms of religious practice in the Hattiantean cities.

At first, worship had not been compulsory. Mother Nunbarshe had issued all sorts of recommendations on how to behave. People had started to laugh at them. The temple and these edicts were the subject of mockery that circulated throughout the city. Issessinak had then created a faction called the "Good Hattianteans", charged with ensuring that these precepts were applied. Its members tracked down and reprimanded "bad" behaviour. They posted lists of "Bad Hattianteans" at the entrances to the markets.

Then they began to ban celebrations. First, those that took place on so-called holy days, so as not to offend the gods with improper revelry. Soon, the ban extended to all festivities in the streets of the city and, eventually, even at home. As people continued to party at home, the Good Hattianteans set up a service to receive reports. By inflicting ever more severe punishments and making reporting mandatory, they ended up creating a climate of mistrust that had corrupted the entire city. Kunisuu had become a hell.

To finance his lavish personal expenses, Issessinak had created special workshops whose products were sold abroad, "To the glory of Enki and Utu" could be read on the pediments. To supply these workshops with labour, the Good Hattianteans criss-crossed the countryside in search of young girls whom they recruited by dangling before them the attractions of life in the city. When the Hattiarina disaster had occurred, Issessinak had understood that it would allow him to definitively bring the entire city under his control. He had closed all the stores and organised draconian rationing, making food the main instrument of his tyranny. He gave it generously to those who served him and he distributed just enough to survive to the others. Even with what I had seen and experienced in the girls' dormitory, I had difficulty believing it. How could what the Hattianteans had spent centuries building so that everyone could live in peace and freedom have been swept away in a few months by the madness of a Matriarch and her General Intendant?

After relating our visit and the disappearance of Theodossis, I asked Nin-Gula to describe the prison to me.

"There are two or maybe three dungeons, I don't know. They are at the end of a very dark corridor. There is only one guard, posted at the entrance. Every day, I bring soup, wine and bread. I put everything on a table in front of the guard, I take the soup tureen from the day before and I leave. I think there is enough food for three or four, depending on what they give each one."

"Do you think I could replace you one evening?"

"I get a replacement when I have to go to the palace to help in the kitchen or to serve. But I have to warn the guard the day before. If you want, I will do it tomorrow evening."

She had offered it to me without hesitation, despite the risks she was taking. She specified:

"The guard is a guy who is not very smart and not really mean. Every time, he looks at my breasts with knowing smiles. I rebuff him, but you, if you want, you will have no trouble distracting him. Afterwards, you will have to manage to get your Achaean back if he is in there."

I would have to wait two more days before I could act. One, for Nin-Gula to warn the guard and an other for me to bring the soup in his place.

The first day, I had to check the accounts of the sales made in Egypt. I could not help but think about ways to neutralise the guard. It prevented me from focusing my attention on the numbers. The smallest addition took me ages. At the end of the day, having been unable to complete my task, I was given ten lashes that reopened the scars from the chief's blows.

The second one, the prospect of taking action in the evening allowed me to concentrate better, despite my back still burning. The prison service was carried out during the service. My absence would perhaps be noticed, but, if I succeeded, we would be out of the city before they had time to react, if I failed it would no longer matter.

§

The prison was a vaulted corridor lit by two torches smoking black. Judging by the smell, it must have been an old wine cellar. Nin-Gula had announced me to the guard, emphasizing my not very shy nature to excite him. He was standing at the only entrance, sitting on a stool, leaning against the wall. He had a dagger tucked into his belt. Beside him, there was a bench in front of a small table with its cutlery, a jug of wine and the soup tureen from the day before. The corridor was a dead end. In the wall opposite the table, I could make out four doors, only the last two of which were closed. The prisoners must be there.

The guard immediately appeared very familiar, inviting me to sit down with pointed glances. I put the food on the table and sat astride the bench, facing him, my legs spread. After a few exchanges of pleasantries, I turned the conversation to the prisoners.

"Do you know why they were imprisoned?"

"No, no one tells me anything. I just have to stop anyone from entering, that's all."

"You didn't ask them?"

"What for? Anyway, I don't have the right to talk to them."

He stared at my crotch intently.

"You're right, we don't care. Pour me a glass of wine."

He sat down on the bench, his gaze intended to be flirtatious.

"Nin-Gula told me about an foreigner."

"There is one whom the others call the Achaean. Issessinak is to see him tomorrow. They say he was furious when he learned that a foreigner had been arrested without telling him."

I spread my legs even wider, giving him a big smile. He tilted his head to get a better look. With all my strength, I smashed the jug of wine on his skull. His head hit the edge of the table and he collapsed onto the bench. I took his dagger away from him. As I stood up to go to the dungeons, he was already coming to. With both hands, using all my weight, I stabbed his dagger into his back. He stood up in one go, taking a loud breath. His eyes bulging, he was trying to grab the dagger. Surprised, I didn't react. He pushed me violently backwards, throwing me against the wall opposite. In a white flash I lost consciousness.

§

I was hearing "Asi! Asi! Is that you?" I could not remember where I was or what I was doing. The guard was on the ground, on all fours, trying to get to the exit. Finding the thread, I grabbed the stool and struck him on the head with it. This time, he fell flat on his face. Theodossis was banging on the door of his cell, calling me. I opened it. There were two men, shaggy, so dirty that it took me a moment to recognise which one was Theodossis. They rushed for the soup and the bread. I pushed the other prisoner away.

"Take what you want and go back to the dungeon."

Theodossis looked at me, surprised.

"We can't leave him outside. We need them to notice your escape as late as possible."

The man was so hungry that he did not protest.

It was almost dark. We ran as fast as we could towards the south gate. With every step it was like someone was hitting me in the head. The few people we passed did not pay us the slightest attention. In Kunisuu, it was better not to notice anything and not to know anything. At the checkpoint we only had to duck under the window where the light was coming from and flee this cursed city.

§

We set off across the fields. Above all, we needed a place to hide and rest. A tiny peasant's hut on the edge of a wood did the trick. Cluttered with useless tools, the roof leaky, it had the advantage of not being visible from the road. Exhausted, shivering, Theodossis no longer reacted. I cleared a corner by pushing the tools as I could and I gathered there all the straw that was more or less dry. Without a word, we laid down, pressed against each other. My head hurt atrociously and my back was burning but I was so relieved that I fell asleep straight away.

The next day, Theodossis told me what had happened.

"As expected, I was able to enter the city easily. I reached the workshop building and hid in a disused shed until nightfall. Afterwards, I had trouble finding the workshop again. The corridors were very dark. I tracked it down by sound and smell. When we visited, they had probably been told to stop working before we came through. There, the hammering on the anvils was deafening. Looking for openings where I could see what they were doing, I entered a storeroom. It was full of weapons: hundreds of swords and daggers on shelves, leather shields and bronze helmets stacked on top of each other, crates full of thousands of arrowheads and spearheads. There is enough to equip an entire army."

"Then it went bad. Some workers came into the store to bring a batch of products. I tried to rush out the back door but there I came face to face with a guard. I claimed to be lost, but he pulled out his dagger and stuck it under my chin. Because of my accent, he had immediately noticed that I was not Hattiantean. He called a colleague and they took me to the prison."

"Yesterday someone came to inform our guard that they were going to pick me up and take me to Issessinak. I think you arrived in time."

Groups of militiamen passed along the road, looking for us. Some ventured into the fields and beat the bushes but without conviction. We stayed two days holed up in our hut, then they seemed to have given up. The rain had almost stopped and the clouds were beginning to let the sun through from time to time. We left for the Vatypetawa farm where our caravan had planned to get supplies. We were hungry and it was urgent to wash ourselves. Theodossis smelled like a goat, I had blood stuck to my hair and my clothes stank of swill.

The farm was located on a hill overlooking the entire region. It formed a real village of at least ten houses clustered around the main house and the farm buildings. Around it, the land had been cleared and put back into cultivation, certainly for quite some time. As soon as we set off on the path that led up to it, three men came out to block our way, armed with pitchforks and pikes. They were very nervous, ready to use their makeshift weapons to force us to turn back. After a long discussion, one of them agreed to go and inform the master of the place. He returned accompanied by a man, armed with a double-edged axe, ostentatiously slipped into his belt. Of an impressive stature, he looked us down, impenetrable. I tried to justify our pitiful state. He listened to me, impassive, showing just a little surprise when I told him that I was from Hattiarina. He let me finish and then, without a word, he motioned for us to follow him. When we arrived at the farm, he gave the three men instructions in a dialect I did not know, then he went back to his work.

We were taken to a woman and her two daughters who gave us food and, above all, water to give us back a human appearance. They told us that, like Lugal-Kahn, their distrust was due to serious troubles they had had with the people of Kunisuu. From the first days after the explosion of Hattiarina, their master had mobilised all his workers to clean the fields. They had managed to keep a good part of their land under cultivation and to save their livestock. Because of this, they had been the object of increasingly violent harassment to force them to deliver their production to Kunisuu. Issessinak had even come in person to propose an Intendant "to help them in these difficult times."

The next day, when we came to greet him and thank him, the master was warmer. He confided his concern to us. He too saw Kunisuu as a threat to the entire Hattiantean people. Because of this, he himself was making weapons with the metal of old agricultural tools. Before letting us go, he had us bring some provisions. His wife insisted on offering us a large blanket and two big woollen hats, warning us of the cold that awaited us in the mountains.

§

THE DAWO DISTRICT

The wife of the master of Vatypetawa had done well to impose her beanies on us. From the first heights of the centre of Kephti, we faced an icy blizzard whose sleet burned our faces. During the hours spent with my head down looking only at the stones in front of my feet, I remembered what we had seen in Kunisuu: the indecently lavish meal, the girls reduced to slavery, the insane cults, the incitements to denunciation, the weapons workshop, the cellars transformed into prisons. For several years, some had seen the increasing glory of our Hittite neighbours as a threat. No one imagined that evil could come from within. After having put the Matriarch under his hold, Issessinak exercised his evil power over Kunisuu without sharing and, by making proposals for alliances, he sought to extend it over the entire island. This had to be prevented at all costs. The other cities, Kamaljia to the northeast, Opsjia to the west and Payto to the south had to ally themselves against him and, regretfully, arm themselves in the same way as him. Between the three of them, they would succeed in eliminating the tyrant and bringing peace back to the Hattiantean land. If only to avenge Ninissina and my own rape, that day, I swore to myself to fight with all my strength against this evil greater than those caused by the explosion of Hattiarina.

After the blizzard, when we had only covered about twenty stadiums, a thick fog immobilised us. We could not take the risk of getting lost. We stayed there for two days, shivering under our blanket, in the impossibility to leave. Instead of one day, the crossing of the mountains took us more than three days, but beyond the last pass, a spectacle that we had not seen for months made us forget our suffering. Under a bright sky, the valley leading to Payto stretched to the horizon, with woods, villages, cultivated fields and cattle grazing in the meadows. On this side of Kephti, very little ash had fallen and the rain of the previous days had finished washing everything away.

§

In the first village we reached, the villagers were preparing a banquet for the remarriage of the master of the community. As was always the case on such occasions, they invited us. For me, it was a move back, not only to the time before the catastrophe but, even further, to my childhood memories. The musicians played tunes long forgotten in Urukinea, and the people danced like I had done as a little girl at the parties given by my parents. The steps came back to my legs as if it were yesterday. Despite our exhaustion, I led Theodossis into these farandoles of a time forever lost. In the early morning, drunk on wine and sleepiness, we collapsed in a corner of the barn for a short hour rest before continuing our journey to Payto. A village festival, blue skies, green meadows, we were emerging from the nightmare we had been struggling with for months.

§

Founded by the first swarming from Hattiarina, Payto was the oldest Hattiantean city in Kephti and certainly one of the most beautiful. Welcoming, buzzing with activity, it was still animated by the spirit of freedom and joy of life of the first settlers. The suburb occupied the entire hillside. To the south, a stadium from the city, a camp had been set up to accommodate refugees from the eastern regions. The caravan led by Sin-Andul had found there those who, after having tried to disembark at Dikta, had continued until Payto. I was happy to see all the survivors thus reunited but an even greater joy awaited me. We were congratulating each other when Sin-Andul appeared, accompanied by two young women. After a moment of disbelief, I felt my legs falter to the point of having to hold on to Theodossis. It was indeed Isthar and Ninlil who were holding out their arms to me. As I rushed to hug them, a terrible emotion overwhelmed me. Since the dreadful story of Hattiarina escape, I had avoided anything that could remind me of my family or my lost friends. The happiness of this reunion reopened the wound.

Unable to control my sobs of pain and joy mixed together, I could no longer detach myself from them. They dragged me aside. With her joy always so contagious, Isthar found the words to make me think of something else and even, by evoking our crazy escapades, make me laugh.

"How did you get to Payto? I asked her."

"After you left, the repairs at our school were endless. Weary of having us at home all day, our parents sent us to Kamaljia, to stay with friends who have children our age. As soon as we arrived, I fell ill. I had a fever and was coughing a lot. Our hostess then sent us to Payto to a friend of hers who was renowned for her medicinal knowledge against this fever."

Pale complexion, drawn features, she still looked tired.

"And you are cured now?"

"Yes, yes, I'm fine."

"Are you sure?"

She quickly changed the subject.

"Do you know what I immediately thought of when Sin-Andul told me you were in Kephti?"

"Tell me…"

"I thought that with all those of Hattiarina, we should found a new city."

They were waiting for me to react. Ninlil continued.

"…And imagine that by listening to people talking here and there, we realised that many of them were thinking about it too."

"You think too much! Of course, we would all like to rebuild a city. But now is not the time. There are still too many uncertainties and threats hanging over the future of Kephti. Come, let us join the others to celebrate our reunion."

§

Sin-Andul had requested an audience with Mother Ninkilim on the question of our installation in the abandoned village. The Matriarch explained to us that it was the city initially created, under the name of Dawo, by the colonists of the first swarming of Hattiarina. Thanks to its port open to Egypt, the colony had experienced very rapid development. The site did not allow for the expansions that had become necessary, so it had been decided to build a new trading centre on the current site of Payto. Over the years, the attraction of the more modern and better equipped facilities had emptied the old city of its inhabitants.

The Matriarch was not surprised by our request. She did not object, but she hastened to call our future village "the Dawo district", thus insisting that it would remain under her authority. She added that, Payto being overloaded, we should take full responsibility for the restoration work. She concluded by designating Sin-Andul as Intendant of this new district.

I continued with Issessinak's proposal for an alliance between Kunisuu, Opsjia and Payto. She reacted strongly.

"I know Issessinak and I don't like him. He has an unhealthy taste for luxury and pomp, he is pretentious and his attentions to the Matriarch are inappropriate. Before the catastrophe, I often went to visit Mother Nunbarshe because of her illness. At that time he had already spoken to me about an alliance between our two cities, "the most powerful in Kephti" according to his own words. This expression was revealing of his ambitions and I did understand that he saw himself at the head of this alliance. I see that he is taking advantage of the situation to bring it up again. But my position has not changed: I will not make any alliance with him. As for Lu-Namhani, the Matriarch of Opsjia, I have only seen her once and that is enough for me to know that I will never get along with her. She is a woman full of herself who despises her people."

I was pleased to see her in this disposition towards Issessinak, but I also wanted to bring her to admit the necessity of equipping her city with an armed force as soon as possible. To show her that he was not only thirsty for luxury and wealth, I described to her what we had seen and experienced at Kunisuu.

"I am surprised by what you tell me about how people would be treated in Kunisuu. Issessinak is nothing but a vain man of no stature. If he makes weapons, it is probably to compensate for his lavish expenses by selling them to the Egyptians or the Achaeans. I cannot believe that it is to turn them against Hattianteans. The Great Federation of Cities is founded on a refusal to use armed force and, until proven otherwise, Kunisuu is part of it."

I insisted, trying to convince her that he was going to face major supply difficulties, and that he would inevitably end up attacking the least affected region, that is to say us. Before I had even finished, in an annoyed tone, she pretended to have other pending matters to end the hearing. I could not convince the Matriarch to mobilise resources against a danger she did not believe in.

§

Despite this very worrying situation, faced with the necessities, our installation in Dawo quickly became our main concern. The buildings were still standing, but most of the roofs and terraces had collapsed. Clogged by vegetation, the sewer system was out of order. Many slabs had been dislodged by roots and the channels were filled with earth and debris. The walls of the small Central House were in good condition but the roof frames had disappeared and an imposing plane tree had flourished right in the middle of the entrance. Only the Central Square, with its row of stalls and its covered market hall still standing, was usable almost as it was.

We were all enthusiastic. The first operation was to allocate the houses. For Theodossis and me, the question was special. We planned to return to Ios but neither he nor I considered leaving Kephti as long as the threat of Issessinak had not been removed. Not knowing how long it would take, it was difficult for us to choose how to settle. Isthar and Ninlil gave us the answer by asking to come and live with us. Postponing our questions until later, we chose a house, not very large, but sufficient for the family they wanted to recreate.

Situated on the edge of a wood, it was overgrown with brambles and broom. We set about clearing it energetically. However, once the initial euphoria had passed, our family project ran out of steam. Still not recovered, Isthar tired quickly, Ninlil was more often with her new lover's family than with us, Theodossis spent more and more time at the port trying to get a fishing boat and I was taken up with the sewers repair project that Sin-Andul had entrusted to me. Fortunately, most of the other families were much more diligent so that in a few weeks our district began to come back to life. Despite a still limited supply, the market was held every morning and, around the Central Square, artisan workshops began to be set up.

Anticipating her future appointment as head of the festivities, Isthar proposed to organise the inauguration of the District House on the occasion of the winter solstice. The work was not finished but the roofs were in good condition and, inside, the bulk of it was done. It was enough to organise festivities. Sin-Andul accepted her proposal. Forgetting her illness, she set to her task with an enthusiasm she had not had for a long time. She regularly came to submit her ideas to me. It was such a joy to see her again in such a good mood that I willingly accompanied her in her fantasies without worrying about the result. Besides, I would have been wrong to do so because the party was a success. She had planned games where everyone had a lot of fun, including a memorable singing contest. In the middle of the night, while I was recovering from a wild dance with her, Sin-Andul came to sit next to me.

"This abandoned village was a blessing for us and you did a remarkable work."

He was searching for his words.

"I am proud to take responsibility for our community…"

He obviously had something else to tell me. He continued.

"… but, like all those of Hattiarina, I would have preferred that we found a new city, … and I believe that we should…"

I interrupted him.

"Today, barely nine months after the disaster, we are all together and we have enough to house and feed ourselves. It is unexpected. The time to found a city may come, but we must first finish restoring our neighbourhood and organise our community. In any case, Mother Ninkilim made it clear to us that we would remain under her Matriarchy. What worries me more is her lack of lucidity about the threat that Issessinak represents. Despite everything we have told her, she refuses to believe it. He will attack us and, if we have not prepared anything, Payto and Dawo will end up under his thumb. Before thinking about founding a city, we must avert this threat. And to do this, we must arm ourselves now."

I motioned for Theodossis to come join us. He had seen the weapons Issessinak was making and I wanted to convince Sin-Andul that we could do the same. He listened to him without interrupting and then said:

"I don't doubt our ability to make weapons, but what would be the point? We have no experience in war. Who will train our officers and soldiers?"

"We have no choice: to protect ourselves, we must speak the same language as him, that of weapons."

"Assuming we succeed, what weight will Dawo's army have against the one Issessinak has been building in secret for months, perhaps years?"

"Let's at least do what we can right now. Whatever happens next, we will have bought time. If we do nothing, Issessinak will be able to come and help himself to our warehouses whenever he wants. Mother Ninkilim will eventually understand it, by herself or by force of circumstance. If we have already made progress on our side, we will be ready to work with Payto to create a real army. We must take action without delay, with or without Mother Ninkilim's consent."

Sin-Andul reacted strongly.

"We cannot do without her consent. We must go to Payto to speak to her."

After the Matriarch's reaction during our last meeting, I was worried about the result of such an approach, but he was right.

§

Against all expectations, Mother Ninkilim was sensitive to our arguments and, although she did not agree with us, she did not oppose our project. She only reminded us that, for this too, we would be limited to our own resources. The essential thing was acquired: we were able to actively prepare ourselves. The very next day, Sin-Andul called a district council to announce the creation of the weapons workshop. He appointed Theodossis in charge and instructed his deputy to organise a collection of all metal objects that were no longer in use or not essential. An old shed outside Dawo was requisitioned.

This new project soon provoked reactions. The restoration work on the quarter was far from finished, the craftsmen were overwhelmed and they feared that they would be deprived of tools and materials that were already difficult to obtain. Sin-Andul and I had to fight to calm tempers and maintain the effort, at the cost of concessions that slowed down the work. Despite it all, at the end of the winter, the workshop was ready and enough metal objects had been gathered to begin the manufacturing which, little by little, took on a regular rhythm if not an intensive one.

I then undertook to visit the farms and villages of Mesaraa in order to recruit our first soldiers. Unfortunately, like their Matriarch, the peasants did not believe in the reality of the danger. There had never been a war in Kephti and they did not imagine that it could happen. I convinced only a ploughman to whom the Master of Vatypetawa had spoken of the aggression of the militiamen of Kunisuu, and Antonis, a former Achaean soldier married to a Hattiantean woman. The ploughman agreed to equip his workers if we provided him with weapons. Antonis understood the situation but, like Sin-

Andul, he immediately pointed out the difficulty posed by our ignorance of military matters. He suggested that, for the training of our soldiers, we call upon the instructors of the Mycenaean army in which he himself had served. According to me, given the exhaustion of our resources, such a costly operation was not conceivable. I asked him if he would agree to train a group of Hattiantean instructors to at least begin our training in war. While persisting in affirming that we would better ask the Mycenaeans to send us instructors, he agreed. Together we resumed a recruitment campaign with a view to forming this first group of cadets. He knew better than I how to find the words to convince the young people of the value of the commitment we were asking of them, so well that, three weeks later, he began to teach the handling of weapons to the only girl and the five boys he had recruited.

§

Over the months, our military organisation became integrated into the life of our district. The recovered metal channels worked better and better, and, observing the exercises taking place in a field outside the village, young people began to take an interest in military action. Theodossis divided his time between the weapons workshop and the refloating of a boat that an old fisherman from Payto had given him, his health no longer allowing him to go out to sea. For my part, I was able to return to the sewers repair works and even help Isthar with the decoration of our house. An ordinary life thus resumed its course, to the point of making us forget the threat that, however, still weighed on us.

One day when the weather was very nice and very cold, I went down to the port to see the boat. Neither the place nor the temperature were conducive to lovemaking, but at home we had little time for ourselves. For once, we had some quietness. The mixture of the icy air and the heat of the sun on the skin finally proved to be quite stimulating. In any case, although a little quick, it was effective. Two months later, between the nausea and the desire to sleep at any time, I understood that I was pregnant. I tried to avoid telling Theodossis before being completely sure but it was no use because he had noticed that my breasts were growing. He was delighted with both: the child to come and the big breasts.

The prospect of birth quickly became our main concern. We gradually settled into our new life as parents, with many arguments, about the arrangement of the room, about education and especially about the name. With a thoughtfulness that I had never known him to have, Theodossis even left his boat to be with me more often. He made wooden toys, pretty but not always suitable for an infant. Ninlil asked a thousand questions about the birth of children and Isthar wove brightly coloured swaddling clothes, "because there was no reason why swaddling clothes should always be white". As in the time of Urukinea, I spent hours with her talking and laughing, especially because of the names she suggested to me, original but impossible to inflict on a child. When her illness was taking over again, she would lie down next to me and put her hand on my stomach. Her cough was calming down and she would fall asleep. I, despite the joy that this coming birth brought me, often had bitter thoughts. We were a few days away from the millennium of the Hattiantean foundation. Instead of being born into a jubilant people, our child was going to grow up under the threat of war.

§

Shortly after the autumn equinox, I gave birth to a pretty little girl, all wrinkled and with lots of black hair. We called her Melina, an Achaean name chosen by her father. Despite the tragedies we had experienced and the threat always present in our minds, it was a happy time. Of course, this feeling was stronger for us but it also animated our entire neighbourhood. Markets, collective meals and festivities once again punctuated the life of our community which, little by little, healed its wounds. Unfortunately, at the beginning of the summer, just two years after the Hattiarina disaster, this sweetness of life came to an end with the arrival of three emissaries from Kamaljia. Mother Ninkilim urgently convened the council so that we could hear them with her.

"The inhabitants of the eastern regions have not managed to put their lands back into cultivation because of the ashes, the lack of water and the diseases. Together with those who had already abandoned Dikta, they have come to swell the refugee camps around Kamaljia. Our city is only surviving at the cost of drastic rationing rigorously organised by Mother Nanshe and her General Intendant. In Kunisuu, on the contrary, Issessinak has not been able to preserve the city's reserves. He rationed the population, but at the same time, all his courtiers helped themself without restraint. The stores were already almost empty by the end of spring. He then attacked the Vatypetawa farm. An Egyptian worker who managed to escape recounted that an armed squadron arrived by surprise, before dawn. They gathered everyone in the courtyard and executed the Master in front of them. Then, they installed an Intendant and plundered the reserves. Two days later, they tried to do the same in Turusa. But the small city had already taken the precaution of preparing its defence. At the cost of a hard battle, they routed the militia of Issessinak."

This heinous murder brought us back to reality abruptly. I blamed myself for having given in to the sweetness of an illusory peace. I felt as if I had betrayed those of Vatypetawa who had rescued us with such generosity.

Her face disfigured by the horror of what she was learning about, Mother Ninkilim did not react. The messenger continued.

"Mother Nanshe has decided to equip herself for our defence, but Kamaljia cannot take on both the burden of the refugees and the creation of an army strong enough to attack Issessinak. She asks that our two cities ally to get rid of him once and for all. Today, he is weakened by his mismanagement of resources, but she fears that he will ally himself with the Matriarch of Opsjia. She could provide him with the food he lacks and, in that case, he would feel strong enough to attack us and you. Before arriving here, we passed through Kalataa and Gortunjia, the two cities located at the entrance to the Mesaraa. They know that they are the first to be threatened. They ask that you help them."

Mother Ninkilim could no longer ignore the danger. Recognizing her mistake, she announced her decision to provide Payto with defences and to help the cities of northern Mesaraa equip themselves. This turnaround would finally allow us to oppose the tyrant with a force that matched the threat. I tried to take advantage of this to return to the case of Opsjia, which she had not wanted to discuss during the first interview.

"Shouldn't we try to convince Mother Lu-Namhani to join us before Issessinak does? Faced with Kamaljia, Payto and Opsjia united, he would be in a position of inferiority."

This time again, she reprimanded me sharply.

"I have already said what I think of Mother Lu-Namhani. Arguing with her will get us nowhere. Let us not waste time. Let us take care of the defence of the Mesaraa. That is already a lot to do."

The next day, she gathered the population in the Central Square. From the balcony that was usually used to launch the festivities, she announced without ceremony to a stunned crowd her decision to create an army. She ordered the construction of workshops on the model of ours and, in order to be able to buy the necessary metals, she asked that the production of everything that was sold in Sukypawu and in

Egypt be increased. Finally, she launched an appeal for volunteers to form the first battalions.

Under the energetic leadership of a Matriarch eager to make up for lost time, the population of Payto mobilised. A few weeks later, their own workshops began producing weapons. Workers came to reinforce us, which allowed us to both expand our workshop and convert a small farm building with a view of the entire Mesaraa into a watch post. Supported by this general movement, the recruitment campaigns that I resumed with Antonis bore fruit. Volunteer soldiers flocked and, thanks to our group of instructors, their training began immediately on the field where bullfights and sports competitions were usually held. By early fall, our army was a reality. Even without Opsjia, the combined efforts of Kamaljia and Payto would allow us to confront Issessinak.

§

Only two months later, events confirmed how indispensable this reaction was. A delegation from Gortunjia came to ask us for help. Kalataa, located a few stadiums to the north, had been taken by Kunisuu. As at Vatypetawa, they had plundered the reserves and imposed an administrator. This was Issessinak's first step towards Mesaraa. The master of Gortunjia was certain that the next attack would be on them. He asked us to provide him with military protection before it was too late. At all costs, we had to prevent Issessinak from continuing his advance on the path that led him directly to

Payto and Dawo. After studying with them the layout of their village, we decided to send them the means to block access to the north of Gortunjia: equipment and two instructors to equip and train the one hundred and fifty soldiers they could provide as well as fifty archers and one hundred and twenty lancers taken from our own forces. They left accompanied by some of our soldiers to prepare the installation of military camps on site.

This operation was the cause of a heated argument between Theodossis and me. Having completed military training, I wanted to fight. Theodossis refused, citing my supposed importance to our village and my role as a mother. I would not budge. I wanted to be present at the battle of Kunisuu and, above all, I hoped to participate in the capture of Issessinak. Overcome by a feeling of humiliation, I lost control of my words. Wounded, he took refuge in complete silence. We did not speak to each other for several days, until Melina fell ill. She cried incessantly, suffering from something we did not understand. Our concern as parents forced us to communicate again and, as if by magic, Melina recovered.

§

During the weeks following the installation of the fortifications in Gortunjia, nothing happened. In Dawo, the streets and the market square, almost deserted, were strangely silent. Then, one day, the expected leavers did not return to the village. The fighting had begun. In a burst of communion, the people gathered every evening under the market hall. To deceive my anxiety, I began to decorate the wall of Melina's room by speaking to Theodossis as if he were in the room. This interminable wait ended on the seventh day at midday when the watchman burst into the Central Square, shouting: "They are coming back, they are alive." We ran to meet them. They were alive indeed, but in what a state! The most valiant walked in front, heads bowed. The others, wounded, were crammed into carts pulled by oxen. Right away I saw that at least a dozen were missing. Luckily, I caught sight of Theodossis. His arm was in a sling, but he was one of those still standing.

We settled the wounded in the communal dining room of the District House. Theodossis had been hit in the arm by an arrow. While I was sewing up his flesh, between two grimaces of pain, he recounted what had happened.

"They were smarter than us. We expected them to come by the road that goes down the mountain. They must have sent scouts because they passed without us seeing them. Then they attacked us by surprise from behind, coming up the flanks. They had more archers than us. They were constantly sending volleys of arrows. We couldn't advance. Then they charged. We resisted but there was a moment of panic among us. They surrounded about ten of our soldiers who had to surrender. We pulled ourselves together and, with the help of those on the eastern flank, we pushed them back. For a day, we remained face to face, a few cubits away, without fighting. When night fell, they simply broke camp and returned to the city with the prisoners. Attacking them in the streets with the troops we had left was impossible. We could only retreat. We lost."

I tried to be encouraging.

"This was our first battle. We will talk about it and learn from it. You will explain everything that needs to be improved."

"Our soldiers have been valiant and our equipment is good, especially our shields. Theirs are too heavy and they did not resist our spears well. We need more archers and above all we must provide many more arrows. We ran out of them too early. But the most serious thing is that we should have secured the interior of Gortunjia and not just try to block its access. Once they were in, there was nothing we could do."

Three dead, seventeen wounded, twelve prisoners and Issessinak who had taken another step towards Payto. The toll was disastrous. This defeat confirmed Antonis's concerns. Whatever the quality of our weapons, it could not compensate for our lack of experience while Issessinak had had plenty of time to train his troops, perhaps even with the help of Egyptian or Hittite advisers.

The next day, a war council brought together Sin-Andul, Theodossis, Antonis, myself and Enmerkar, the General Intendant of Payto. We were in the middle of discussing the different possibilities to stop Issessinak's advance in the Mesaraa when an assistant of Enmerkar burst into the room. Mother Ninkilim was asking us to join her in her office. She was waiting for us there in the presence of a man.

"This is Payata. He comes from Opsjia where he is a wine merchant. He arrived this morning with his whole family asking us for asylum. He will explain to you why."

"A little over a week ago, Mother Lu-Namhani gathered everyone in the Central Square. She explained that the people of Kunisuu were at risk of starvation due to poor harvests and the ravages of rising waters on their coast. Afterwards, she announced that under the pact of the Great Federation, she had granted Mother Nunbarshe's request for help and that as a result she was forced to impose rationing on us until Kunisuu had replenished its reserves. We all accepted out of solidarity with the people of Kunisuu."

We didn't see where he was going with this.

"Go on, Payata", said Mother Ninkilim.

"Yesterday, on my way to my vineyards, I came across a cart that had broken a wheel. Helping them pulling their cart to the side of the road, I saw the load. It was shields, helmets, and spears. The carters refused to give me any explanations, but I understood what was happening. Opsjia is arming itself. Mother Lu-Namhani is using our city's reserves to buy weapons. The people of Opsjia think they are safe from Issessinak's madness. They are wrong. I do not want my children to live in a city where militias arrest people in the street and everyone watches everyone else. I add that I have not only come to ask for asylum. I also want to fight alongside you."

Issessinak had launched the attack in the direction of Mesaraa because he had managed to solve his food problem and to gain a military ally. When Opsjia would be sufficiently armed, nothing would be able any more to prevent him from enslaving all of Kephti. This alliance was the final blow. Antonis intervened.

"Kunisuu has been militarily equipped for a long time and is connected by road with its ally Opsjia. In the face of this, our army is just beginning to exist and we are isolated from our ally, Kamaljia. Attacking the Kunisuu-Opsjia alliance is now beyond our strength. The only thing we could do would be to try to block access to Mesaraa."

"That is to say, let three-quarters of Kephti fall under the yoke of Issessinak, added Mother Ninkilim. We cannot be content to barricade ourselves and abandon Kamaljia. We must fight."

Sin-Andul suggested that we concentrate all our forces only on Gortunjia, attacking as quickly as possible.

Antonis continued.

"Even if we managed to retake Gortunjia, Issessinak would eventually enter Messaraa, on the Opsjia side for example. At first, I suggested that we call on Mycenaean instructors for our military training. Now, I see that it would not have been enough and that only calling on a strong and experienced army fighting at our side can allow us to defeat Issessinak. Mycenae has such an army and, thanks to King Furumark, the city is at peace at present."

To my surprise, Mother Ninkilim did not reject this possibility.

"From the lands of Arsawa to those of Elam, Furumark and his army are feared by all. Perhaps this would be a solution."

I argued.

"The Mycenaean army could perhaps provide us with decisive support, but I cannot see how we could pay them for an operation of such magnitude."

"You are right, but from what Antonis says I understand that, alone, we will exhaust ourselves without managing to eliminate Issessinak. I think we have no choice."

Enmerkar then raised the possibility of negotiating with Issessinak a division of the island in exchange for guarantees of non-aggression on his part. Mother Ninkilim and I were convinced that no agreement with such a deceiver could have guaranteed anything. The Matriarch categorically rejected any idea of compromise with him. She continued.

"I believe we must first contact King Furumark to see if he might agree to help us. The question of our means will come later. We have no time to lose. I must convene the city council to decide."

The council met that same evening. Mother Ninkilim asked Antonis to give them a detailed account of the military situation. They immediately rejected the principle of a foreign army intervening on Hattiantean soil, considering that it would be very difficult to ensure that it would leave Kephti. After our arguments, some of them reversed their position by also mentioning the possibility of negotiating with Issessinak. The discussions continued all night. Mother Ninkilim listened to the arguments of each side without intervening, then, in the early morning, she interrupted the debates.

"I am certain that no negotiation is possible with Issessinak. He would break his word as soon as the agreement is signed. On the other hand, I share your concerns about the risks that the intervention of the Mycenaean army on our land would entail. However, for the moment, we do not even know if King Furumark would be willing to help us and, if he could, we do not know when or under what conditions it would be possible. Issessinak will soon take advantage of the current situation. We must move forward. I propose to send a delegation to the King of Mycenae. We will know if he agrees to help us and what he asks in return. We will then judge the risks that this entails and we will make our decision. Let those who are opposed to this approach speak now."

The Matriarch looked around the assembly. No one reacted.

"Perfect! We must therefore form the delegation that will go to Mycenae. If she accepts, I would like Asiraa to lead this delegation. It seems to me that she is the right person for this. She was the first to alert us to the seriousness of the threat posed by Issessinak and she has repeatedly demonstrated her negotiating skills. If she agrees, she will represent the four Matriarchs of the free cities of Kephti: Kamaljia, Chaminjia, Dikta and Payto, with the title of Ambassador of the Great Federation. She will therefore first have to go to Kamaljia to obtain the approval of Mother Nanshe and the Matriarchs of Chaminjia and Dikta who reside there. She will be accompanied by our General Intendant, Enmerkar, whom I ask to prepare this embassy without delay, under her instructions. If no one has any questions, ... This advice is over."

As the participants left, Mother Ninkilim motioned for me to stay.

"Forgive this informal appointment. I did not want to waste time holding another council. It is a heavy responsibility, but I am confident in your ability to carry it out."

"Your trust honours me, Mother, and it is with pride that I accept this mission. I will do my best to be worthy of it."

"I have no doubt about it. I wanted to talk to you about a question that I preferred not to address in council to avoid rekindling the debates. We do not have the means to pay the king, but we can perhaps interest him in another way. Shortly after his enthronement, he came to visit the Matriarchs of the Great Federation. He spoke to us then of his wish to develop trade between the Achaeans and the Hattianteans. Since then, he has never returned to Kephti but I think you could speak to him about it again. I had noted in particular that he was interested in our relations with the Egyptians. We could offer to open the way for him in that direction. You will have to pay attention to understand what could decide him to come to our aid. But time is pressing. We cannot afford several trips back and forth to Mycenae. You will therefore have to commit us from this first embassy on the compensations that we are prepared to offer him."

"I understand. What kind of man is Furumark?"

"He is... attractive! Well, seductive, mostly. A little too much for my taste. You will judge for yourself but be on your guard, he is also a king who never loses sight of the interests of his people or his own."

"I will only return with his promise to help us eliminate Issessinak."

"You will also have to bring gifts. I thought of purple. Our workshops are renowned for producing the most beautiful shades, of a quality that has nothing to envy to that of the city of Tyre. You will also take embroidered dresses. They are very popular with the Achaeans. The king will be delighted to be able to offer them to the ladies of his court."

"I would also like to make a request."

"Yes ?"

"I would like my companion to be the one who takes us to Mycenae."

"Of course. Go! And may the spirit of Queen Nanaya watch over you."

The following days were all the more exhausting because the prospect of having to leave Melina made me anxious. We spent as much time as possible with her. Two days before our departure, we isolated to find ourselves all three at home. I was able to take the time to explain to her what was happening and why we were going to have to leave. The last day, I took a nap with her in a hammock. Full, she was sleeping on my chest. I felt like she wanted to go back into my belly and come with us.

§

FURUMARK

Enmerkar had many questions about our embassy. How were we going to get an audience with the king? What would he ask of us in exchange for his help? What absolutely had to be refused? How many soldiers should we ask of him? I tried to explain to him that it was best not to anticipate too much, but he would not stop. He only ceased talking when we passed the southeastern tip of Kephti. A rough sea with an almost headwind made sailing very uncomfortable. Looking concentrated, he was visibly turning paler and paler. Just as I was about to suggest that he move to the leeward side, he shot across the boat like an arrow to vomit overboard while clinging to the rail. For the next two days we spent tacking along the coast, he never left the gunwale, his nose flush with the waves.

When we arrived within sight of the port of Kamaljia, two boats came to meet us. They were equipped with a bronze spur on the prow and their crew was armed. After forcing us to give long explanations about the reasons for our visit, they escorted us to the port where armed soldiers took us to the harbor master's office. The war that Queen Nanaya fled had well and truly arrived in Hattiantean land. After two hours of waiting during which Enmerkar regained a more or less normal complexion, an escort came to pick us up and take us to Mother Nanshe. Since our last visit, the refugee camp had doubled in size. Just leaving the port, we could already see huts on either side of the road, increasingly close together as we approached the city.

§

Drawn features and grey hair, Mother Nanshe appeared to have aged several years. I explained to her the purpose of our visit.

"King Furumark has a reputation as an excellent warlord. With his help, we could undoubtedly defeat Issessinak. But he will certainly demand significant compensation. How do you intend to pay him? We are overwhelmed by the influx of refugees. The harvests are very insufficient and our artisans do not produce enough to meet our needs. I must warn you that we will not be able to contribute."

"Payto will not be able to offer anything either. Even though it is less affected than you, it has also taken in many refugees. We plan to interest the king by offering commercial advantages to the Mycenaeans and helping them sell in Egypt and Sukypawu."

As did some in Payto, the General Intendant of Kamaljia objected that, by bringing the Mycenaean army to our land, we risked seeing it settle permanently. Mother Nanshe anticipated my reaction

"That's true, but with Issessinak, it's not a risk that we're talking about. It's the certainty that hell will fall on the Hattiantean people. I agree with Mother Ninkilim. Let's see what the king proposes to us. At worst, he'll turn Asiraa away, and we'll be back to where we are today. On the contrary, if she manages to convince him, we can eliminate the tyrant. That's the most important thing. After that…"

She was raising both hands to mean "Come what may!"

During the rest of the interview, she explained to us that, since the attack on Vatypetawa, Issessinak had been keeping his militias at a distance. He had realised that Kamaljia was well armed and that its population had tripled. The task must have seemed too big to him. But, with Opsjia's help, she had no doubt that he would end up feeling strong enough to return to the attack. As we parted, she confided to me:

"Be wary of Furumark. Don't be duped."

The next day, a meeting was held with the Matriarchs of Chaminjia and Dikta who were staying at Kamaljia. Young and inexperienced, they rallied to Mother Nanshe's advice. Once the three seals were affixed to the papyrus next to that of Mother Ninkilim, we set sail for Mycenae without further delay.

§

Theodossis assigned Enmerkar to the trolling lines. He taught him how to set the bait, how to unwind the line without tangling it, and how to watch it carefully so that a shark or barracuda would not steal a catch. Enmerkar took this mission to heart, which had two positive effects. He no longer felt seasick, and he stopped talking. He quickly got the hang of it, regularly bringing in fish that he cut up himself and put out to dry in the sun.

After eight days of exhausting navigation, we finally arrived at Kios, the port of Mycenae. It was the same bustle, the same festival of colours and noises as at Aphaia. Like there, we could see the series of taverns with their flowery terraces and the waitresses laughing at the sailors' hackneyed jokes. In Kephti, all that had disappeared. Even in Kommo, the port of Payto, most of the taverns had closed. People were too busy or too tired to come there to divert themselves. In those that remained open, all they talked about was the difficulties of fishing, the cold, the diseases and the threatening war.

At the harbour master's office, when we told them that we were coming from Kephti to meet the king, they did not believe us. During the explosion, they had seen the column of smoke and heard the most violent detonations. Afterwards, they had not encountered any more Hattianteans boats and sailors said that they no longer saw Hattiarina. Rumours then spread, claiming that the Hattianteans had been engulfed by the waters. We had tried to explain to them what was going on, but they remained all the more suspicious of our intentions especially because of the presence of an Achaean with us. They sent us away.

"The king will not receive you. You should have sent emissaries first to request an audience."

Back on the boat, dejected, I watched people come and go, when a cart stopped at our height to unload. The donkey harnessed to it had the same white muzzle and the same circles around its eyes as Waspi.

"Anything wrong with my donkey?"

Lost in my thoughts, I didn't realise how surprising it was that someone was speaking to me in Hattiantean. I answered in kind.

"No! I have a she-ass that resembles him and I'm sure she would like him a lot"

The carter returned to the Achaean.

"Oh! You speak too fast. It's been a long time since I last spoke Hattiantean."

"Where did you learn our language?"

"I lived with a Hattiantean for ten years. When she was in a bad mood, she would rant and rave in Hattiantean. So, of course, I learned."

"It seemed to happen to her often."

"All the time! That's why we're not together anymore."

"And me, how did you know that I was Hattiantean?"

"Since that time, I recognise a Hattiantean at a hundred stadiums."

"And you run away?"

"Not always. Some are very attractive…"

"Beware, my companion is Achaean. You are well placed to know that the Achaeans are jealous."

He greeted Theodossis who was already scowling.

"Where are you from? I thought the Hattianteans were all dead."

"Hattiarina has been buried under the ashes and part of Kephti was ravaged but, as you see, we have not disappeared. We just need help and that is what I have come to ask your king for. We must go to Mycenae to see him."

"Just that! And you think he will receive you."

"Of course he will."

"And how do you plan to get to Mycenae?"

"I don't know. Till now we're trying to recover from our trip."

"The road is long. On foot, with your luggage, you will not be able to arrive before nightfall. I am going back there. I have some bales to load and then I can take you. There will be enough room in the cart."

I accepted without hesitation. While Enmerkar and Theodossis collapsed on the bales of hemp, I sat on the bench next to Stavros, our carter. I hoped to get some information about Furumark but it was in vain. He spoke only of his countless conquests. I tried to bring the conversation back to the king but he always returned to his exploits. Finally, tired of my lack of enthusiasm, he stopped talking. I had only learned that the king was rather well-liked by the population and that he regularly organised events to glorify his great achievements.

§

The citadel of Mycenae was located at the top of a spur, at the foot of the high mountains that bordered the valley. Surrounded by an imposing blind wall, it was austere, almost disturbing. Outside the fortifications, the slopes of the hill were occupied by an immense suburb. I became aware of the lack of preparation of our expedition. Without thinking about it, I had assumed that we would be able to go directly to the king's residence where we would be received without further formality. Here, the world was divided in two: the suburb, outside the enclosure, and the royal citadel, inside. We were outside and I did not even know where to access inside.

Our donkey was progressing steadily through the tangle of alleys. Arriving at a small square, he stopped. In the middle, an imposing stone pine stood, under which an inn had set up its tables. Stavros woke us from our torpor.

"Here we are. I live here."

We had almost nothing left to eat and nowhere to sleep. The best thing would have been to go straight to the palace. I asked Stavros where we could enter the citadel.

"You have to go to one of the three gates, present a safe-conduct and pay the toll. As for going to the palace, I don't know how that works. You'll have to ask at the guard post but you can't do anything before tomorrow morning. Come, I'll offer you a beer at my brother's inn. He has rooms for passing traders. I'll ask him if he has any available. At worst, you'll sleep in the cart. Wait for me here, I'll talk to him."

Enmerkar was exasperated to see me improvising that much. I tried to sound confident that the letter with the four seals would give us easy access to the king, but it infuriated him. He complained that after an exhausting journey we ended up nowhere, forced to sleep in a cart, with nothing to eat. The two brothers returned.

"Stavros explained your situation to me. I do have a spare room, but I can't give it to you for nothing."

"We only have the gifts intended for the king: wine, embroidered robes, saffron and purple. We had not planned to stay in the city. We thought we would be received at the palace today."

"Keep your gifts. You will not be able to present yourself to the king empty-handed. I will let you have the room for tonight, but afterward you will have to vacate it."

"Thank you. We can at least rest. I am sure that tomorrow our embassy letter will allow us to access the citadel. I can still give you some saffron, if you need it for your cooking."

"Don't worry about my cooking. But don't believe it too much. It's very difficult to get into the citadel. It will take you days just to get a safe-conduct. In addition, I believe the king has gone hunting in the mountains. Usually, it lasts at least a week. I have a proposition to make to you, but I'm afraid it might offend you."

"Your turn, don't worry about me. I want to meet the king. Tell me…"

"I need a waitress. If you're interested, I'll offer you room and board in exchange."

It was an unexpected stroke of luck. We would be able to make our requests for safe conduct and an audience while waiting for the king's return. Enmerkar lost his temper. He would not accept that an Ambassador of the Great Federation would work as a waitress in an Achaean tavern. I explained to him that no one would know who I was, but he continued to shout in Hattiantean, drawing the attention of the entire place to us. Theodossis, for his part, found it very amusing. He was delighted at the idea of finally being able to put his hand on the waitress's buttocks without getting a slap. I advised him not to try.

Before my first day of work, we went to one of the gates of the citadel to understand how it was going. Closed with a heavy portcullis, it was severely guarded. I asked the provost if we could obtain an audience with the king, insisting on my status as Ambassador of the Matriarchs of Kephti. At first suspicious, he finally agreed to record our request for an audience. All this took the whole morning, to get him to confirm that the king was absent, and that we would have an answer in about ten days. Back at the inn, I wanted only to lock myself in the room and see no one anymore but the innkeeper was getting impatient. Returning from the fields and fishing, customers were flocking.

Stavros' brother was a warm man, so much so that his inn was frequented by warm people. Very quickly, as a surviving Hattiantean, I became the curiosity of the neighbourhood and he understood how to take advantage of it. He asked me to do my service dressed in one of the embroidered dresses I had told him about. His idea turned out to be an excellent one. The terrace was always full and I was having a lot of fun, much to Enmerkar's despair.

§

When the king returned from hunting, the news of his company's arrival at the entrance to the suburb emptied the inn in one go. Assembled along the main street, the curious jostled to get as close as possible. Drowned in this crowd of people taller than me, I couldn't see anything. Suddenly, the clatter of the hooves covered the noise of the street. Standing on tiptoe, I saw him for a brief moment, enough to single him out without hesitation: his haughty bearing made him appear higher on his horse than the other riders. He was gazing at his people with an imperceptible smile of satisfaction.

Seeing the king in the flesh gave us hope. Enmerkar went to the toll booth every morning to get news of our request. After a week, the provost informed him that we would be received by a "rawateka", the equivalent of a Hattiantean General Intendant according to what the people at the inn explained to me. Although this reminded me of the bad memory of the forced visit to Kunisuu, we had no choice. We were escorted to administrative buildings, where the rawateka received us immediately. Contrary to what I feared, he carefully read the letter signed by the four Matriarchs. He asked me for details on the status of the signatories and the state of our armed forces. He promised to deliver the letter to the king, while specifying that he was very busy with the major construction of his mausoleum. I tried to stress the urgency of our situation. He interrupted me with a wave of his hand and ended the interview by asking us to wait until a messenger was sent.

I had been very presumptuous in believing that we would be received immediately by the king, on the sole faith of our titles. This succession of hopes and disappointments was exhausting. At the inn, the customers saw that I was not well. Tired of having to keep up appearances, I decided to explain to them who I really was and why we had come to Mycenae. They were shocked that their king did not react. The next day, they returned with their family and friends. The square was packed with people. As I watched them discuss among themselves the king's attitude and assail Theodossis and Enmerkar with questions, an idea came to me. Armed with a cauldron and a large wooden spoon, I climbed onto a table, drumming on the cauldron. I said to them:

"Achaean friends, nature has inflicted immense disasters on the Hattiantean people. Hattiarina has been wiped out. In Kephti, the ashes and rising waters have devastated half the island. Livestock have died in the fields. The sun no longer makes crops grow or fruits ripen. In winter, the plains are covered in snow and water freezes in the streets and houses. But the worst is that one of us, the filthy Issessinak, wants to take advantage of this to enslave the Hattiantean people to his tyranny. He has already subjugated the city of Kunisuu and is secretly equipping an army to bring the entire island under his control. He is a traitor who no longer deserves the name of Hattiantean."

"You are attached to your freedom. A people is losing its own. Can you let them fall into servitude without reacting? You have a good king, who has made your city prosperous and who preserves you from war. Help me convince him to come to the aid of the Hattianteans."

After a moment of hesitation, a man jumped onto the table next to me and shouted:

"Asiraa is right. This tyrant is a threat to us as well. Our king maintains at great expense an army larger than necessary. He must send it to Kephti to put Issessinak out of harm's way."

Screams rang out from all sides.

"Let's help Asiraa! Let's free Kephti!"

These reactions thrilled me.

"Let's go to the guard post to request an audience with the king."

They followed us as one man. There were dozens of them shouting: "An audience, an audience!" As we walked towards the guard post, a man came up to me.

"You need more people. Follow me, we will go to all the inns in the city. You will speak to them as you did under the stone pine and we will take them to the toll."

All afternoon, we toured the inns. Each time, we left with more people. As we passed through the streets, people were coming out of their houses. We explained to them what was happening and many more came to swell the ranks. We arrived in front of the tollhouse at nightfall. They were shouting: "An audience, an audience!" The guard came out of his casemate, followed by the provost. Dumbfounded, they looked at the crowd gathered in front of the door they were in charge of. The provost gave an order to the guard who immediately disappeared. He shouted "Silence! Silence!" to no avail. Only the arrival of a battalion, lances pointed forward, finally allowed him to speak.

"What's going on? What do you want?"

"An audience for Asiraa!" someone shouted.

I was at the foot of the stairs. He recognised me.

"You again? You've been told to wait for the king's answer. If you hope to settle your affairs by causing chaos, you are mistaken."

He continued, addressing the crowd.

"Asiraa's request has been forwarded to the king. He will give his answer later. In the meantime, disperse! Go home or I'll order the guards to charge."

He gestured to the soldiers. They stepped forward, threatening the crowd with their spears. The demonstrators in front stepped back, pushing the others aside. A woman shouted:

"No! He must receive her now."

Another added:

"We are not afraid of your spears! We will not leave. Go tell the king that we are here and that we will stay until he hears from Princess Asiraa."

Shouts flew, approving of the women's injunction. The provost hesitated.

"I will refer this to the rawateka. In the meantime, go home. Anyone who approaches the door will be executed."

Despite his threats, the crowd remained in the square. The nearest inhabitants brought food and drink, and then some came with their musical instruments, transforming the riot into a joyous festival. Those who were around me soon asked me to sing them a Hattiantean song. In Hattiarina, I never wanted to sing in public. That evening, carried by their fervor, I climbed the stairs leading to the door and, with all my soul, I sang in an impressive silence the refrain in praise of the Great Federation of Hattiantean cities. Theodossis and Enmerkar could not get over it.

§

Early in the morning, the craftsmen who were supposed to go to work in the citadel flocked to the square, causing a general commotion. The carts could no longer manoeuvre and goods of all kinds were piled up everywhere. The craftsmen were getting impatient. Panicked, the guards no longer knew whether it was better to let them pass, or to risk a riot by respecting the instructions. The provost returned.

"This gate is closed on my orders. If you have a safe conduct to enter the citadel, go to one of the other two gates."

This announcement triggered enormous confusion. Some attacked my supporters, ordering them to flee. Others attacked the provost, ordering him to open the gate. My supporters demanded that the king himself come. The square became a free-for-all from which no one could escape because of the tangle of carts. The insults flew, more and more heated. Enmerkar and the man who had guided us from inn to inn wanted to take me to safety. On the contrary, I joined the provost at the top of the steps. I suggested that I ask my supporters to stand back to let those who had a safe conduct pass, and, as a guarantee, I agreed to accept arrest if there were any incidents.

"We'll see. Shut them up and let me talk."

I motioned for the crowd to be quiet. The provost spoke.

"Here is what I have decided. All those who have no business in the citadel will move as far aside as possible so that the others can enter. We will check all the safe conducts. I want peace and order. Princess Asiraa will remain here during this time. At the slightest attempt to force the way in, I will have the gate closed and I will arrest her."

I added:

"I came in the name of the Hattiantean people to ask for help from your army, not to prevent you from working. Your support is an honour for me and for all the Hattiantean people. I trust you and I am sure that, thanks to you, I will be received by the king."

In less than an hour, all those who had the right were able to pass through the gate. Then, my supporters reinvested the square.

In the afternoon, tempers began to flare again. The crowd grew louder and shouts of "We want to see the king!" and "An audience for the princess!" rang out again. Around the guardhouse, there was a feverish agitation. From time to time, the provost appeared at the top of the steps. Nervously, he looked around the square. Finally, a guard came down to get me and take me to the provost.

"The king will receive you, but the people must first evacuate the place. Tell them to go home. If they do, I will take you to the palace. The king wants you to come alone."

I was sure that I would obtain the evacuation of the place without difficulty. On the other hand, I did not understand why the king wanted to see me alone. There was no question of Enmerkar and Theodossis not coming with me. Fearing sanctions against him, the provost categorically refused. I insisted, arguing that as an official delegation we could not be separated under any circumstances. He would not budge. I finally obtained permission for Enmerkar to accompany me, swearing to him that I would make it clear to the king that it was against his will. I had a lot of trouble calming Theodossis down.

§

The royal palace was extraordinarily lavish. One entered it through a passage opening onto an immense square courtyard bordered by a colonnade and refreshed by four basins supplied with running water. At the end of this courtyard, a monumental staircase led to the upper floor. There, we were introduced into a bright audience hall, furnished with a richly decorated throne. Furumark entered, accompanied by a person who was speaking to him, doubtless reminding him of the object of this interview. He listened to him while staring at me. I noticed that he too had blue eyes.

"Welcome, Queen of the Hattianteans, and accept my apologies for the hassle you have been subjected to."

"You receive me now and it is a great honour for which I am grateful. But know that I am not a queen. My name is Asiraa. I present myself before you as Ambassador of the Great Federation of Cities of Kephti. I am accompanied by Enmerkar who represents the Matriarch of the city of Payto who is at the initiative of this embassy."

Furumark greeted Enmerkar absently. He took me by the hand to make me sit down. Leaving his throne, he sat down opposite me and, with a gesture, he invited Enmerkar to do the same.

"I know that the Hattianteans have no queen. I always thought it was a shame, and now that I see you, I know I was right. Besides, the Mycenaeans were not mistaken either. Your arrival in Mycenae did not go unnoticed. They say we grazed a riot. Is it usual for the Hattianteans to cause such disorder when arriving in a foreign city?"

"My turn to apologise to you, Great King. The distress of our people and the urgency to help them may have made me lose my sense of proportion."

"Don't apologise. The Hattiantean people are very lucky to have you as their… ambassador."

"This praise flatters me."

"Let's get to the point. The rumours about the disappearance of the Hattianteans seem unfounded. I'm glad, but I guess you didn't come all this way just to let me know."

While I was explaining in detail the consequences of the Hattiarina explosion, I could realise how much Furumark, despite his show-off air, was paying close attention to his affairs. He often interrupted me to ask for clarification or to give his point of view. When I mentioned Kunisuu, he reacted.

"Before the explosion of your island, this Issessinak had contacted weapons manufacturers in Mycenae. Surprised that Hattianteans would want to buy weapons and because he did not inspire trust to them, they came to inform me. On my advice, they refrained from dealing with him."

When I came to the battle of Gortunjia and its disastrous outcome, Furumark gave an instruction to his aide-de-camp and then interrupted me.

"I understand what is happening and I see where you are going with this. I have asked for the rawateka of the armies to be brought. We will study how we can help you. I know Kephti. It is a magnificent land and I will not let Issessinak seize it."

He was smiling at me thoughtfully.

"You impress me, Asiraa. What courage, after all you have endured. And what audacity to come and force my door to ask for help for your people! It is a woman like you that I would want for queen."

"Why look so far? I'm sure there are many Mycenaean women who could satisfy you."

"The idea of a foreign queen would not displease me."

"Then come to the aid of the Hattianteans. You might meet the one who suits you."

"Isn't it already done?"

His nonchalance irritated me as much as my difficulty in hiding my impulses.

The leader of the armies entered. Powerful in stature, with a broad neck and a drooping mouth, he looked at me with contempt before greeting me, his gaze shifty.

"Take a seat, Iorgos. This is Asiraa, ambassador of the Great Federation of Hattiantean Cities."

To my surprise at the accuracy of this presentation, Furumark responded with a mocking look that, in spite of myself, made me smile. Enmerkar noticed. Furumark quickly summarised the situation to his rawateka before asking his opinion on the possibilities of intervention of the Mycenaean army. Iorgos addressed the king as if we were not there.

"Thanks to you, great King, the kingdom is at peace. I think we could consider mobilizing part of our army for such an operation. But Kephti is far away. It will be very costly and…"

I interrupted him, addressing Furumark directly as well.

"Our granaries are empty, all the workshops in the eastern cities are at a standstill. In Kamaljia and Payto, the artisans cannot produce enough to cover the needs of the inhabitants and refugees. I must tell you: we will not be able to pay you for a long time."

Furumark didn't expect such a direct statement. He hesitated a moment before reacting.

"So be it! Then how am I going to justify to my people that we weaken our defence and risk the lives of our soldiers across the seas?"

"The Mycenaeans have much to gain from this. The Hattianteans are better craftsmen and better traders than you. They cast the best bronze, they weave fabrics whose finesse is recognised beyond the seas, they cultivate saffron and they produce purple. They will teach you this and they will bring your merchants to Egypt and to Sukypawu. Your people will enrich themselves by coming to free Kephti."

Iorgos intervened.

"These are just words. Once Issessinak is eliminated, the Hattianteans will only worry about themselves. We will only be able to repatriate our troops and mourn our dead."

I handed him the papyrus bearing the seals of the Matriarchs.

"All the Hattiantean people will be grateful to the Mycenaeans and you have the commitment of the Great Federation. We will keep our promises."

"If you don't keep them, we will have no way of forcing you to do so."

He addressed the king again.

"The spoils of war can never compensate for the costs of such an operation. We need more. I suggest that the Great Federation cede us territories."

I was taken aback. Such a request was unacceptable, but I could not find the words to dismiss it without compromising everything. Enmerkar was fuming. Furumark was waiting for my reaction. The rawateka spoke in his ear.

"Iorgos wants to speak to me one-on-one."

As soon as we were alone, Enmerkar reproached me for having revealed too quickly our inability to pay him, for not consulting him and, above all, for having fallen under Furumark's spell. The king returned alone. He seemed upset.

"Iorgos had to go back to the staff meeting from which I had taken him. He wanted to give me details on the risks of a landing at Kephti."

Iorgos' absence allowed me to regain my senses a little, but I did not understand what had happened between them. He continued.

"I have no illusions: the Hattiantean people will never pay us and I will not be able to wage war on them to force them to do so. So, rather than territories, here is what I ask: the Great Federation should agree to allow us to set up a trading post in Kephti. We will build a port and warehouses there and it will serve as a relay point to the Hattiantean cities, Sukipawu and Egypt."

"We did not consider this possibility before we left. Therefore, today, I cannot answer you on behalf of the Great Federation, but as far as I am concerned, I approve of it. It will bring our peoples closer together and enrich the Mycenaeans. I will present it to the Great Federation and I undertake to obtain the agreement of the Matriarchs."

Enmerkar intervened in Hattiantean. He disapproved of this commitment made without prior consultation with the

Matriarchs. I did not want to discuss it but he insisted. I had to order him to shut up and not to contradict me in front of Furumark.

"I don't need to understand your language to realise that it won't be as easy as you say. No matter. I believe you're capable of convincing the other Matriarchs and I'm sure the Mycenaean people will benefit from it. But what about me? What will I have to gain?"

"Glory. In Mycenae, in a hundred years, you will still be spoken of as the king who opened the way to Kephti and Egypt for the Achaeans. In Kephti you will be honoured as the great king who freed the Hattiantean people from tyranny."

"And if it goes wrong, I'll be the king who led his army into a disastrous adventure."

"It is a risk, indeed. But you will know how to avoid it. That is why we are calling on you."

With a doubtful pout, he made me understand that I was overdoing it.

"Even though I trust you, I will not engage the Mycenaean army on your word alone. Iorgos will go to Kephti as soon as possible to ensure the commitment of the other cities to the installation of a trading post in Kephti. If they agree, he will prepare with you our landing in Kephti."

The audience had lasted until dusk. Before leaving, Furumark suggested that we join the meal he was to have with a few notables. Once the kingdom's affairs were settled, his seductive nature immediately took over. Under Enmerkar's dark gaze, I spent the entire meal laughing at the colourful anecdotes he delighted in about each of his guests, never missing an opportunity to place his hand on my arm, and even on my knee.

§

The journey back to Kephti seemed interminable, as I was so eager to see Melina again. As soon as we disembarked, I rushed to her nurse's. When she saw me, she turned her back on me and screamed. She sulked for a moment, refusing to look at me when I tried to approach her. Once she had taken her revenge, she finally accepted my hugs with tenderness.

The next day, we reported our embassy to the council of Payto. Mother Ninkilim was initially reluctant to grant the Mycenaeans the right to establish a trading post in Kephti. To my great surprise, Enmerkar was the first to defend my position. He argued that it was better to leave them a well-defined territory rather than risk seeing them settle wherever they pleased without our control. Some members of the council were sensitive to this argument, but Mother Ninkilim stuck to her position. I intervened.

"Since the Hattiantean founding, we have rejected any foreign presence on our soil for fear that the war we fled would return. This attitude has not protected us. Nothing compels the Mycenaeans to come and help us. If they do, will we treat them as enemies? The inhabitants of Mycenae supported me. The king himself told me of his determination not to let

Kephti fall under the tyrant's thumb. Do you think they will wage war on us? On the contrary, I am convinced that this commercial port will be the continuation of the momentum that animates them today."

"Once the tyranny is defeated, we will have a huge task ahead of us to rebuild the cities of the East. Our populations are already very weakened by restrictions and diseases. The cooperation of the Mycenaeans will not be too much, and by associating with their traders, we will revive our own trade more quickly."

Finally, after a long debate, Mother Ninkilim closed the council without having changed her mind.

"I need some time. I will make my decision within a few days. In the meantime, I am instructing Enmerkar to organise a mission to Kamaljia without delay to gather the opinions of the other three free cities."

On the way out, I asked Enmerkar about the turnaround of his opinion. He admitted to me that he had thought about it during the return from Mycenae and had realised how unexpected what we had obtained was.

§

Two days later, when the mission to Kamaljia had just left, we were surprised to see two Mycenaean boats docking at Kommo. Mother Ninkilim summoned me to the Central House.

"How come they're already landing? Where are we with Kamaljia?"

"The mission is on its way. It will be back in four or five days because it has to go by the eastern route to avoid Kunisuu."

"Truly, cohabitation with the Mycenaeans already looks to be quite difficult. I still don't know what to decide, and they are forcing our hand. Let us not show ourselves to be hesitant. You will tell Iorgos that I agree and that we will soon have confirmation from the other cities. That will save us time."

True to form, without any prior politeness, Iorgos set up his camp on the shore. Instead of questioning us about the decision of the Great Federation, he immediately asked that we present to him the geographical configurations and the situation of the different cities, complaining that we had not prepared plans before his arrival. I gave him those of the surroundings and the main streets of Kamaljia and Kunisuu but I did not know Opsjia. Although it represented a difficulty at least as important as Kunisuu, we had to be content with the summary indications of a merchant who went there regularly. For long hours, we reported on the plans all the distances as well as an estimate of the populations in the different districts. Three locations were chosen for the landing of the Mycenaean army: one to the south, on the large beach where the plain of Mesaraa ends, and two on the northern coast. The aim was to take Opsjia and Kunisuu in a pincer movement between the Mycenaean contingent reinforced by our own army to the south, and the two other Mycenaean contingents attacking to the north. Iorgos estimated that it would take between two and three months to mobilise these resources. An eternity.

The next day, he wanted to inspect the workshops and weapons stores, then review a contingent of our army. Since he still had not inquired about the Matriarchs' position on the installation of the Mycenaean trading post, I took the lead by informing him of Mother Ninkilim's. After a moment of hesitation, he said:

"If I remember correctly, there should have been a response from other cities as well. What about it?"

"We have sent emissaries to Kamaljia to get the approval of the other three Matriarchs. We will have the answer in four days, five at the most."

He got angry, saying he had to leave the next day, and again reproaching us for our lack of preparation. I feared he would postpone or even cancel the operation.

"To avoid Kunisuu, the emissaries had to take a difficult and longer route. But we are certain of their agreement. We vouch for it."

I expected him to brush this assurance aside. He simply said "Anyway, it's not my responsibility. I'll tell the king what it is all about and he'll decide."

It was surprising but it was enough for me. I was certain of Furumark's decision.

Two days after Iorgos' departure, the delegation led by Enmerkar returned from Kamaljia with the agreement of the three Matriarchs. Like us, Mother Nanshe had prioritised the restoration of peace and freedom. Concerning the installation of a Mycenaean trading post, she was even more favorable than Mother Ninkilim, seeing advantages for the prosperity of Kephti.

Everything was in place. The prospect of seeing avenged the suffering endured by the girls of Kunisuu, by Ninissina and by me gave me great satisfaction, almost joy.

§

THE HUNT

Ninlil was the first to see them from the terrace of our house where we were enjoying the mildness of the late afternoon.
"Over there! Look at all the boats on the sea."
Hugging Theodossis, I watched through my tears as these little dots grew imperceptibly on the horizon. We didn't need to recognise their sails to know where they came from. Judging by the number of ships, there must have been between two and three thousand men. It was much more than expected. The main landings were to take place on the northern coast while, for our part, we were only waiting for reinforcements for our own army.
The fleet stopped at sea, leaving the command boat to continue to shore. I had hoped to see Furumark disembark. It was Iorgos. With a closed air, he abruptly inquired about the location we had planned for their installation. Suspecting him of wanting to confine us to a secondary role, I demanded an explanation of the reason for such an armed force on our coast. Unfortunately, it was not a ruse. As soon as he returned to Mycenae, the rawateka had sent observers around Kunisuu

and its ally Opsjia. Two weeks before his departure, he had learned that, as Mother Nanshe feared, Issessinak had attacked Kamaljia. Having failed to take it, he was now besieging it. Along the way, he had captured the small city of Turusa so that he now controlled access to the northern shores. Landing at both of the originally planned locations would have been suicidal. Iorgos and Furumark had then decided that the king would land in a single place, much further west, and that part of his troops would arrive from the south with those of Iorgos. Our entire strategy had to be reviewed. Furumark would not be able to attack Opsjia and Kunisuu at the same time, we could no longer count on the forces of Kamaljia now under siege, and the installation of Iorgos would take longer than expected while we wanted to take Issessinak by surprise.

§

Five weeks later, Iorgos' troops and our own army finally went on the attack. Two Mycenaean divisions accompanied by a Hattiantean battalion set off for Opsjia, while a division composed of equal numbers of Hattiantean and Mycenaean soldiers marched towards Gortunjia, with a view to retaking it before moving up towards Turusa and Kunisuu. Eager to take revenge for the defeat at Gortunjia, Theodossis set off with them. As for me, even if I had agreed not to expose myself directly to combat, I still could not imagine staying in Dawo, just waiting to be informed of the fall of the tyrant. I decided to form a rescue team to follow the armies into the field. My role as a mother may have prevented me from fighting but certainly not from rescuing those who were risking their lives for our freedom. With a few volunteers, we collected eucalyptus decoctions and saffron ointments, as well as everything that could be used to sew, cut, clean and make splints. Once this material was loaded onto Waspi, we left for Gortunjia, where the first battle was taking place.

When we arrived on site, our soldiers had already entered the city. The commander of the operation had taken over a house to set up his headquarters. Slumped on a couch, sword still in hand, he listened to my explanations, his gaze in the distance.

"You are full of good intentions, Asiraa, but you are unconscious. Where you want to go, there are no more human beings to rescue. There are only wild beasts killing each other, driven by nothing but hatred and the thirst for revenge. Believe me: forget your generous idea, go back to Dawo and wait for us to finish our work."

While I was making him understand that this was out of the question, he had a glass of wine served to him.

"As you wish. But I warn you, I will not risk the lives of my men to come to your aid."

He indicated me a place where the battle was raging. In a square, about twenty soldiers from our camp were facing those of Issessinak entrenched in the adjacent alleys. He had spoken the truth: mixed with the din of weapons, the roars we heard were not human. At our feet, corpses, torn limbs, dying men. It smelled of blood, flesh, excrement. Several of us vomited. The crack of an arrow lodged in a door near the head of a young woman brought us out of our stupor. We rushed into an abandoned shop. A second arrow wounded Waspi, who we were unable to push inside. Once we were safe, we organised ourselves. Rugs and curtains found upstairs to make beds, large bronze dishes piled up at the back of the shop to protect us while we went to get the wounded and drag them under cover, a brand heated red to cauterise wounds. The fighters quickly understood what we were doing. Soon, our infirmary overflowed into the neighbouring houses.

We were proud to rescue our soldiers, but it was a thankless mission. Those who recovered went back to fight as soon as they felt sufficiently valiant, and, despite all that we did, young men left in our arms, in terrible suffering. Each of us worked hard at our task, avoiding thinking and pretending not to see those who, on the verge of discouragement, went to cry in secret.

After three weeks of fighting, at the cost of much destruction and loss of life, the battle of Gortunjia ended with the defeat of the enemy army. For a year, Issessinak had been gaining ground. For the first time, we forced him to take a step back and showed him that his army was not invincible. The commander placed a garrison in the north to prevent any attempt by enemy troops to return, then he appointed one of his men as governor of the small city to ensure its security. I would have preferred a Hattiantean, but events were moving quickly and there was no time for discussion. Before leaving with his troops to join those of Furumark, he came in person to our dispensary to seize the enemy soldiers we had treated. Even if they had betrayed, they were still Hattianteans who had the right to be judged according to our principles. As I protested, he simply reminded me that I could still buy them before they are shipped off to be sold in the Mycenaean slave market. As if that were not enough, Theodossis came the same day to tell me that he was leaving to continue fighting at Turusa.

§

After landing on the northern beaches, Furumark had taken up position in front of Opsjia. Hoping to see him again, I took our rescue team there. When we arrived, the enemy troops were massed outside the city, facing the Mycenaean troops to the north and south. There was no fighting. Furumark was waiting for the contingents he had sent to Turusa to return. As soon as he learned that I was there, he came to the dispensary. Leading his army on the battlefield, he was in his element. Serene, he displayed a reassuring confidence. He helped us set up our rescue unit, providing us with tents, beds and cooking equipment, and requisitioning canteens.

The situation remained frozen for a fortnight, with the armies camped face to face, little more than an arrow's throw away. The king often invited me to the dinners he had with his staff. The brotherhood that united these soldiers and their willingness to ignore the dangers and horrors of their daily lives made these evenings joyful. All you could hear was jokes, songs, and bursts of laughter. For the duration of a meal, they were becoming human beings again. One evening, I stayed after the officers had left to talk to Furumark about the fate of the enemy soldiers. He confirmed to me that he could not and would not do anything. The generals derived a large part of their income from the sale of defeated soldiers. Depriving them of it would have discredited him. I expected this reaction, but I wanted to try.

There was no one left with us. He led me out to a hill overlooking the valley. In front of us, lit by the moon, the enormous mass of Mount Psilowitis stood out against the black sky. He wanted to tell me the real reason why he had agreed to our request for help. He imagined what he called an empire, uniting the Achaeans and the Hattianteans, encompassing the territories of Mycenae and Argos as well as all the islands from the far north to Kephti. And, of course, he wanted to create it with me. He was seeing me spreading the spirit and knowledge of the Hattiantean people throughout the empire, while he would ensure its security and expansion to other territories. As he described it, it seemed so simple that one could not help but believe it. I was convinced that he was really capable of it. That we were capable of it.

He stopped talking. All we could hear was the stubborn screeching of an insect. Taken by the coolness of the night, I had curled up on myself. Putting his arm around my shoulder to let me benefit from his warmth, he leaned down to kiss me. The moment of waiting for the contact of his lips on mine was enough to ignite my desire. I abandoned myself with voluptuousness to this kiss then to the more and more intimate caresses that accompanied it, until his increasing breathing suddenly made me aware of what I was doing. My excitement died down but I no longer had the strength to escape his. Delighted, I let him reach his ecstasy. Afterwards, he said: "It will be better next time." For me, there could be no question of a next time even if, despite the remorse that was already assailing me, I had enjoyed making love with him that night.

§

A messenger finally came from Turusa to announce the victory. Two divisions were on their way to provide support against Opsjia. The enemy reacted immediately by engaging in combat before they arrived, triggering the greatest battle of this fratricidal war. It lasted four months during which, day and night, we repaired, stitched and amputated, kicking away the crows that came to eat in the wounds. Four months during which I too had to abandon my humanity. I no longer felt anything. I no longer even sensed the smell of blood and carrion. Whenever I could, I would go and hide in a small room in the dispensary to think about Theodossis and Melina, clinging to the hope that we would soon be reunited. War had always intrigued me by the self-sacrifice and courage it was supposed to inspire. I had no idea that the reality was such a horror. Issessinak had awakened the worst in the human soul in both camps. Even in me, he finally stirred up a hatred and a desire to kill that made me ashamed.

The battle turned to our advantage. It ended with several days of fierce fighting around the Central House where Mother Lu-Namhani was entrenched. The soldiers tried to capture her, but she struggled like a fury and, in the confusion, she received a mortal blow. This event precipitated the surrender of the few soldiers who were still resisting. For a few hours, the city remained inert, devoured by the dozens of fires started on the orders of the Matriarch in the neighbourhoods that her troops abandoned. Then, the inhabitants came out of the basements of the houses. Distraught, they did not understand what was happening to them. After having suffered the oppression of their own rulers, they saw themselves invaded by a foreign army. We had difficulty convincing them of our good intentions, some even blaming us for having caused the destruction of their city.

The worst part was the children. They were everywhere, wandering the streets looking for their parents and for food, or hiding in corners trying to escape the madness of the adults. The battle had been won, but what was left of the great city? Burned ruins, distraught families, lost and starving children. All because of one man's thirst for power.

One day, I was brought some three or four-year-old twins found in the rubble of a burned-out house. Protected by a tangle of beams, they had escaped death, but not their parents. Clinging to each other, mute, they refused to eat. The bolder of the two had just begun to accept my spoonful of mush when a man appeared in the doorway. Because of the fighting, even on his days off, Theodossis had never been able to join me at the dispensary. I had not seen him since he left Gortunjia. His curls were glistening in the backlight. Leaving the spoon in the little one's mouth, I threw myself on him, nearly knocking him over. It was only when I saw the twin in tears, the spoon still in his mouth, that I resigned myself to releasing Theodossis from my embrace.

The king stayed in Opsjia, the time to get his troops back in combat order before marching on Kunisuu. I had made it clear to him that, regardless of my feelings for him, there was no question of us making love again. Despite this, he never missed an opportunity to come back to the charge and continue to ask me to become his queen. This flattering courtship did not displease me, but he continued to come to the dispensary. Tense, Theodossis remained on his guard, making a scene every time he thought he had caught a suspicious gesture or word. Furumark, for his part, prudently avoided any situation that he felt could turn sour. Actually, they had many traits in common and, apart from the seductive behaviour that Theodossis could not stand in Furumark, I was convinced that they could have gotten along. Nevertheless, the departure of the king with his army to take up position in Kunisuu was a relief. We stayed in Opsjia, the time to place the last orphans and to be able to spend a few days alone.

§

I was eager to leave for Kunisuu where the battle I had expected for almost two years would finally take place. The king had kept himself informed day by day of the enemy troop movements around Kamaljia, waiting to see if, as he had hoped, Issessinak would thin his siege to strengthen his defence at Kunisuu. This was not the case. On the contrary, the tyrant sent reinforcements to Kamaljia, then, breaking the siege, he went on the attack. Despite a valiant resistance from Mother Nanshe's forces, he managed to enter the city and impose himself there. Instead of concentrating his forces on Kunisuu and abandoning Kamaljia, he had taken control of both cities.

The king launched the attack on Kunisuu as soon as he had confirmation that the contingents returning from Opsjia and Turusa were in combat positions. Against all expectations, the battle progressed easily. Few in number, the enemy fighters put up mediocre resistance. They were only trying to delay our troops as much as possible by lighting fires in the quarters they lost. As in Opsjia, according to a plan prepared in advance, they had placed large jars of oil in the streets which they broke and set on fire before retreating. Nevertheless, Kunisuu was liberated in only two weeks.

The Central House was empty, obviously deserted for a long time. Mother Nunbarshe and her governess were found in a small shack attached to the main building. This easy victory had a reason: there was nothing left to defend in Kunisuu. Issessinak was no longer there. A soldier from his personal guard questioned by the Mycenaeans confirmed that he had left for Kamaljia well before the arrival of the Mycenaean army. The fire tactic was only intended to delay us to give him time to organise. Knowing that he was being hunted, he prepared a way out each time. He was slipping through our fingers like an eel. Was he going to escape us and never pay for his crimes ? Although Furumark assured me that this changed nothing, I was beginning to despair of one day seeing in his eyes the fury of humiliation.

With the bulk of the enemy troops entrenched inside Kamaljia, Furumark felt that a direct attack was no longer an option. He feared that the price to pay for victory would be too high, both for our armies and for the city itself. He believed that Issessinak would not hesitate to fight to the end, even if it meant dragging his army and the entire city into his own ruin. He then decided to lay siege to the city. The inhabitants would continue to endure the deprivations they had already suffered for months, but he was convinced that the enemy troops, exhausted and at the end of their resources, would eventually surrender without a fight.

Knowing that the siege would last, the king suggested that we return to Dawo. I missed Melina very much. We were a few days away from her second birthday and, of course, I would have liked to celebrate it with her. But I absolutely wanted to take part in the capture of Issessinak. With Theodossis, who also had a debt to make the tyrant pay, I took our medical staff to Kamaljia shortly after the king left.

§

Although Theodossis had returned to his contingent, the king came to see me only once, towards the end of the third month. Pale, drawn, he appeared tired. After leaving him alone the time to give instructions to free myself, when I returned I found him sound asleep on a stretcher. When he woke up, I expressed my concern about his condition. He simply claimed to have slept very little for several days. When I insisted, he retorted:

"Don't worry, I'll be able to rest soon. Issessinak won't hold out much longer. His absurd attempt to barricade himself shows that he was in dire straits when he left Kunisuu. He's caught in the trap he built himself."

Two weeks later, in a final burst, the enemy army attempted a sortie in all directions at once. Exhausted, its soldiers could not withstand the counterattacks of the Mycenaeans and the Hattianteans. Most surrendered almost without a fight, the others retreated, returning to the city. Our soldiers entered it and put out the last resistance. Kamaljia was liberated with few losses and without destruction but at the cost of indescribable suffering for its inhabitants and for the refugees trapped with them. Corpses rotted in the streets and in the houses, spreading a pestilential odour. In rags, the survivors were of a thinness than I would never have thought possible. The ablest wandered, searching every nook and cranny for food. The others, sitting or lying on the ground, watched us pass without reaction. This time again, the children were the first victims of this horror. How could I forget their eyes, made too big by their cachexia, which were asking us: "Why are you doing this to us?"

Furumark summoned me to the Central House. When his soldiers entered, there was no defense guarding it, and inside, there was only Mother Nanshe and her maid. Skeletal, exhausted, the Matriarch was bedridden. It was she who consoled me:

"It's over, Asiraa. Don't cry. We're going to get our city back on its feet and forget this nightmare."

She informed us that Issessinak and his entourage had disappeared more than a week before. The rumour of his run away had caused the desertion of many of his soldiers. In a rage, I asked the king to send a detachment after him.

"Kamaljia is completely surrounded. All comings and goings are controlled. He is still in the city and he will not leave. We will find him and I will deliver him to you."

When I told Theodossis about this situation, he reacted the same way I did:

"We can't just sit back and do nothing. He will hole up and wait for the Mycenaeans to leave. After that, he will find a way to slip out of the city and disappear."

He was pacing back and forth, mumbling.

"I'm going to investigate the city. He must have accomplices. I'll end up spotting something."

§

With impressive willpower, Mother Nanshe found enough strength within a few days to resume running her city. She asked me to assist her, while she found the successor to her General Intendant, killed during the capture of the Central House by the enemy. The king mobilised his army to bring supplies from the other cities and to put the defeated soldiers to work. Like Opsjia and Kunisuu, Kamaljia came back to life, eager to forget the dark hours. But the days passed and Issessinak remained untraceable. Theodossis was not making any progress and, on the side of the Mycenaean headquarters where I went regularly, I was always asked to be patient, assuring me that they would eventually flush him out. Finally, exasperated, I demanded to speak to Furumark in person. I was then told that he had been in Dawrometo for a week to organise the departure of his troops. On his return, I told him of my doubts about the Mycenaeans' determination to arrest Issessinak, and regretted that Theodossis had been forced to go and investigate on his own. He took my suspicion very badly. The discussion that followed was so heated that he had to sit down to collect himself. His face was closed and pale.

"Forgive me" I said, "I lost my temper because I'm afraid Issessinak will escape us. He has betrayed the Hattiantean people. We can live in peace again only after we have arrested and judged him."

With his head tilted, he looked at me from below.

"What will you do with him? They say you don't condemn to death."

"Nothing prevents us from doing so. We can take life if necessary. The Matriarchs will judge whether this is the case or not."

"And you, what do you think?"

"For me, banishment would not guarantee our safety and, above all, it would not allow us to forget what one of us has done to the Hattiantean people. I think it will be necessary to put him to death."

He gave an order to his aide-de-camp. After long minutes of waiting without a word, an officer entered.

"Let me introduce you to Aktoras. He leads the detachment that is tracking down Issessinak. Aktoras, this is Asiraa, future queen of the Hattianteans. From today on, you will take your orders from her and report to her."

Aktoras turned to me and nodded in agreement. The king continued.

"I admit that I have neglected the importance of this arrest for the Hattianteans. It is better that you take charge of it. The fate of Issessinak is now in your hands."

§

Aktoras had scattered informants throughout the city hoping to obtain information that would betray the fugitive's presence. However, the inhabitants were wary of these Mycenaeans whose presence in their neighbourhoods they did not understand. It was necessary to use Hattiantean informants. With the help of Mother Nanshe, we gathered enough of them so that no neighbourhood escaped us. A month later, this tactic bore fruit. An informant reported that a fisherman, known for his regular visits to taverns, was in the process of repairing his boat that was languishing at the bottom of the harbour. When questioned about the reasons for his renewed interest in navigation, he claimed to have decided to go and start a new life in the land of Lukka. That Issessinak had chosen both this destination and this idle sailor to organise his escape was more than likely. We reinforced our team of informants at the port and Theodossis took it upon himself to make contact with the sailor.

Even before drink diminished his abilities, the fisherman had the reputation of neither a good sailor nor a very courageous man. Theodossis began to tell anyone who would listen about the terrible navigational perils he had encountered on his many, and imaginary, crossings to Lukka. His descriptions of reef causeways with violent currents and waves breaking in sprays of foam had the desired effect. One evening when he was dining alone in an inn, the man approached him. He had come to ask for advice on how to get through the reefs.

"It's a difficult sailing. Many times, I thought my last hour had come. Alone, you might really struggle."

"I won't be alone. A rich merchant asked me to take him there for his business. He pays me well."

"He is not a sailor. He will be of no help to you in navigation. Take some oars. He may know how to use them to fight against the currents. And tell him to take on as little commodities as possible. If your boat is too loaded, you will not pass."

"I don't think he has much to take with him. But you're right, I'll make sure."

"Also, be careful not to arrive at night. Alone at the manoeuvre, you have to see well."

"The merchant wants absolute discretion. He asked me to leave and arrive at night."

"Ow! In that case, don't delay. The weather is calm at the moment and it's almost a full moon. Take advantage of it."

"That's what I planned. I'm leaving in two days, before dawn."

"You've put all the chances on your side. I wish you good luck."

"Above all, don't tell anyone about it."

"Sure, don't worry."

We immediately contacted the head of the warehouses to organise our trap. The day before their departure, Aktoras posted his men in the building bordering the quay. To prevent any escape from the water, Theodossis and a soldier hid in a boat moored near the sailor's boat. Aktoras and I took cover in a tiny counter, just in front of the boat.

Little by little, the sailors and dockers deserted the docks. Night fell. Through the window, I could see only the stars in an inky black sky. With wide eyes, I searched the darkness for the slightest movement. A cat fight made me jump.

"Don't be impatient, he will come", Aktoras whispered.

An hour later, the sailor arrived. The moon was already shining brightly enough for us to see him bustling about on deck, then disappearing into the hold. Once again, apart from the rats that came and went, the quay was deserted. What if it was a decoy? While we were keeping watch in front of this boat, Issessinak might have been quietly leaving the city by road. He was smart enough to have set up a false trail.

Hours passed. The full moon was now lighting up the entire quay. Suddenly, the appearance of two men out of nowhere put us on alert, but their shouting rather made us fear that they would ruin the operation. These drunken sailors disappeared as they had come and the interminable wait resumed. I was starting to doze off when Aktoras took my arm.

"Here he comes!"

A silhouette was emerging from the shadows at the end of the dock. Holding my breath, watching for any sign of hesitation, I counted the distance he had left to travel. When he reached the ship, the sailor came out of his hold and climbed onto the quay. They talked to each other then they stepped onto the gangway. Aktoras raised his whistle to his mouth to start the assault but Issessinak stopped. I thought my heart was going to jump out of my chest. Slowly, he turned around and returned to the quay.

"What's going on?" Aktoras whispered.

On the gangway, the sailor was not reacting. Issessinak remained motionless for a few moments and then, suddenly, he rushed towards one of the warehouse doors.

"Blast it! He smelled something. He mustn't come out again."
Aktoras rushed inside the building, yelling at his men to block the exits. Theodossis and the soldier climbed onto the platform to neutralise Issessinak's accomplice. Going out to join them, a small double-edged axe hanging on the wall caught my eye. I grabbed it.

The soldier questioned the sailor. He explained that he had cursed the boat anchored near his because it would hinder him when getting away from the quay. Issessinak had reproached him for having moored there. He had defended himself by specifying that the boat was not there the day before. Issessinak had then seen ripples sparkling around the boat. He had understood that someone had moved inside. Aktoras arrived.

"All the doors are guarded. He's still inside, but this warehouse is the perfect place to hide. We're going to have a hard time flushing him out. Let's hurry. The port will soon be back in business and we won't be able to block the exits any more."

We spread out across the width of the building to scour it. The interior was a succession of stores, sometimes large rooms cluttered with merchandise, sometimes corridors leading to several cubby holes. With this multitude of hiding places, with only the light of our torches and the moonlight coming from the skylights, we could pass within an inch of him without seeing him. We walked the entire length of the building four times, in vain. The sky was beginning to whiten in the east and the first dockers were arriving on the platform.

We were reaching the end of our last sweep when a soldier signalled to Aktoras. A bale of wool seemed to have been tipped over deliberately to hide the entrance to a staircase leading to a basement. Aktoras, a soldier, Theodossis and I went down it, leaving a guard at the top. At the bottom of the staircase, two corridors plunged on either side into complete darkness. Aktoras went off on one side with the soldier, Theodossis and I on the other. The corridor gave access to small cellars. Only the idea that Issessinak could escape us gave me the courage to enter these pitch-black rooms. Several times, the shadows cast by my torch on the walls made me jump. Suddenly, I heard screams and the sound of a struggle. I went back. Light was coming from one of the cellars. I rushed. Issessinak was about to strike Theodossis, on the ground, curled up on himself. He stopped his gesture.
"You?"
He burst out laughing nervously.
"Enki and Utu are with me. I will send you both to hell."
I couldn't take my eyes off the bloody dagger.
"You see the blood of your companion. Come, come closer so I can mix yours with it."
"You are the one who will go to hell. This cellar is the only palace you deserve. You will pay for your betrayal."
He took a step forward. I screamed, in both rage and terror. My axe struck him full in the face. He dropped his dagger. He tried to speak but, his jaw shattered, he could only utter unintelligible grunts. Stunned, I was watching as if absent from myself, with no memory of having thrown the axe.

Aktoras entered accompanied by the soldier. While they were restraining him, I rushed towards Theodossis. He was choking, holding his stomach. He murmured.

"You got him, you got him."

"Don't talk. Show me your wound."

Yelling in pain, he managed to turn around. He had a deep wound on his left side. I tore open an old hemp sack to make a ball of lint and put it in the wound.

"Push on it as hard as you can. I'll find a way to get you out of this rat hole."

"We'll pull him up" said Aktoras, "and have him taken to the dispensary. In the meantime, watch Issessinak. If he moves, slit his throat."

Issessinak was disfigured. His cheek hung bloody, revealing his teeth. I pulled his skin and jaw back into place, holding them together with a strip of hemp. He was staring at me like a mad dog, wriggling around trying to free himself from his bonds.

"This time it's the end. Your gods have abandoned you. In a few days, you will appear before your judges and all those you tortured and killed will be avenged."

Looking at this pitiful monster, I felt neither joy nor hatred. He did not deserve another moment of my attention.

With the help of two soldiers, Aktoras pulled up Issessinak who now seemed close to losing consciousness. Outside, the rising sun was illuminating the docks already crowded with the hustle and bustle of dockers loading and unloading the boats.

When we arrived at Kamaljia, the rumour had preceded us. A crowd was waiting for us at the entrance to the city, shouting its hatred and throwing stones and shards at the cart where the tyrant lay. All the way to the Central House, the soldiers had to push people back with their spears to prevent them from dismembering him on the spot.

We did not have to bother to judge him. His facial wounds became gangrenous and, despite the care he received, he died two weeks after his capture. His body, hung by his feet, was displayed in the Central Square. The inhabitants demanded that he be thrown immediately to the vultures, so disgusting was the spectacle. We all wanted to forget as quickly as possible both the monster himself and the harm he had done us.

§

ISSASARA

While Theodossis recovered, we had to stay in Kamaljia. As in Opsjia, I took the opportunity to take care of the lost children. New ones were brought to us every day. It was endless and it left me very little time for Theodossis who, immobilised, was getting bored. Finally, although he could hardly get up, he took advantage of the departure of a Hattiantean battalion to return to Dawo beside Melina. Tired of hearing the children whine all day and eager to join them, I was starting to organise myself to leave when Furumark asked me to join him at his headquarters. He was probably looking to be alone with me again, but I felt capable of resisting his advances and I too wanted to see him again.

When I arrived, he was in a meeting with his officers and it was going badly. You could hear him throughout the building. As he entered the room where I was waiting for him, still red with anger, he sank into an armchair. Out of breath, it took him a moment to collect himself.

"My queen! Thank you for responding to my invitation, beauty among the black heads."

"I guess I should take that as a compliment. But you seem very upset. Who put you in this state?"

"I had given orders for the divisions remaining in Kunisuu to withdraw to Dawrometo, as did those of Opsjia and Kamaljia. Their presence in the city is badly received by the inhabitants. I want our army to return to Mycenae as quickly as possible. But Iorgos "did not have time to deal with it". As if he had anything else to do than carry out my orders! I can't stand him anymore. I will get rid of him as soon as he returns to Mycenae."

"If you brought me here to get my opinion on this, I assure you: I won't be the one to stop you."

"I have something else to ask you."

"Not to marry you, I hope. Otherwise, you know my answer."

"Who knows what the future holds? But that's not the point either. Opsjia is run by one of Iorgos' men. I want a Hattiantean matriarchy to be re-established as soon as possible. It's not my role to do that, and besides, I have to go to Mycenae. My construction site is at a standstill. I'm leaving the day after tomorrow for at least two or three weeks."

"Based on her age, Mother Lu-Namhani must have designated the one who should succeed her."

"Before the war, she had approached two young women. She didn't say which one she would choose but, in any case, they are much too inexperienced. In the state the city is in, we need someone solid, not a novice... Someone like you, for example."

"I don't think this would be a good idea. First, I will meet the two girls the Matriarch had designated. Then we'll see."

"Think about it: they have no experience; if you choose one, you will be the only one who can give her the training she will need. This will take months. From this point, to take the place yourself…"

In a world like his where kings seize cities, willingly or by force, he would have been right. I reminded him that in Hattiantean land, a Matriarch does not install herself at the head of a city she does not know and where no one knows her.

He insisted:

"With two cities destroyed by the war and two more buried under the ashes, I'm not sure all your rules still apply. You could do a lot for the Hattiantean people by taking over a great city like Opsjia. And remember our plans: that would be the first step."

"I cannot handle this by myself. It is up to the four active Matriarchs to decide. I will speak to Mother Ninkilim."

He persisted in trying to convince me. He maintained that a single authority on Kephti would be the best solution to raise it and to animate the relations between our two peoples. Such a challenge to the principle of the Great Federation seemed unthinkable to me. Of course, he hastened to crown me Queen of Kephti. If that still did not please me, he managed to disturb me by giving me a very realistic description of our future empire. When it was time to part, he returned to more romantic attentions that I expected and which I affectionately turned down. He made me promise to think about it during his absence and, for his part, he promised me to return quickly so that we could continue building our empire.

Before he left, he ordered a squadron that was returning to the Achaean camp of Mesaraa to accompany me back to Dawo. Alone and comfortably installed, I could at last think of something other than the war and its desolations. Without realizing it, we had become accustomed to this hell. From one emergency to the next, we existed only in the present moment. But tyranny was defeated and the war was well and truly over. "War is over!" I had to repeat these words to myself to force myself to believe it. For the first time in four years, we had a future again.

§

I was climbing the last few cubits of the path leading to Dawo, smiling in spite of myself. Just a few more steps and I would find Melina, Theodossis, my cousins and all the others. As I passed, I was surprised to see the watch house that we had set up before the war cheerfully decorated. I immediately recognised Ishtar's paw.

In the village, the streets were as decorated as the guard post, but the welcome from the people I passed was strange. They greeted me kindly, saying they were delighted to see me back but without any more effusion. When I tried to speak to them, they cut the conversation short. At home, I first found Isthar and Ninlil playing with Melina in the garden. They rushed towards me. Melina pushed her aunts away forcefully so that I could take her in my arms. I questioned Isthar about the behavior of the villagers. She did not answer.

"Have you noticed all the decorations I've put up?"

"Once again, you have done wonders. It is magnificent. But..."

"We are preparing a big celebration for the liberation. We've been waiting for you impatiently. No one would have wanted to start without you. Have you met Sin-Andul?"

"Not yet."

"You have to go see him. He asked us to tell you as soon as you arrived."

Theodossis was resting upstairs. He appeared, emaciated but smiling and in much better condition than in Kamaljia.

"Four women around you! You won't be bored" I told him.

"I hope they take good care of me."

He also added:

"Isthar told you? You have to go see Sin-Andul. I think it's urgent."

"What is urgent is that we enjoy ourselves. I'll see him tomorrow."

In the evening, we discussed the question of our return to Ios. Before the explosion, we had planned to settle in Hattiarina. It was convenient for our respective occupations and close enough to Ios for us to see Theodossis' family. Then, when we had left for Kephti, we had thought of returning to settle in Ios. Now, with the community of Urukinea gathered in Dawo and with Furumark's plans, I did not know what to think.

Everything remained to be done. I could hardly imagine abandoning what we had struggled so hard to rebuild. On the other hand, I feared that it would be difficult for Theodossis to settle so far from his family. Yet, he himself told me:

"I think we should stay in Kephti. In Ios, you will be bored and in the long run you will blame me for forcing you to stay there. You have a much better future here, in Dawo, near a big city like Payto."

"And what about you?"

"For me, the sea is the same everywhere."

"Aren't you afraid of settling in a foreign land and far from your family?"

"I am not really in a foreign land any more, you know. My brothers in arms are Hattianteans. As for my family, with Isthar and Ninlil, I have some here too. Ios is not that far. We can go there and my parents can come see us."

He was sincere, but I felt like he wasn't telling the whole story.

The next day, I went to Payto, accompanied by Sin-Andul. He claimed not to know why Mother Ninkilim wanted to see us before launching the festivities.

"I was impatient to see you, Asiraa. We could not celebrate the victory without our heroine. Because you are indeed our heroine. Thanks to you the Great Federation of Hattiantean Cities will live again."

"I thank you, Mother. It is true that I have put all my strength against the tyrant, but I think especially of the Hattiantean and Achaean soldiers who gave their lives so that we could regain our freedom. They are our heroes."

"I see that the war has not changed you. So much the better! But here is why I brought you here. When they learned of the end of Issessinak, the survivors of Hattiarina sent me a delegation. They wanted to discuss the possibility of founding a new city on the domain of Payto."

I had no doubt who was behind this move. Despite her whimsical nature, Isthar never gave up on her ideas. Mother Ninkilim continued.

"With admirable courage, they gathered together, they rebuilt their homes and they are living in community again. Now they want to ward off the fate that has befallen them by reviving their city. I understand them and I wish to grant their request. Rather than building a new city, I proposed to them to emancipate the Dawo district to make it a matriarchy in its own right."

I began to understand people's behaviour when I arrived. After all these years, fate was going to ask me the same question again.

"They accepted. Then, of course, I asked them who they wanted to choose as Matriarch."

In an instant, I was sent back to Urukinea, to Mother Innana's office, staring at the frieze, my stomach in knots.

"They know who they owe to be there. So, they want you to continue to guide them on the path you put them on."

At the time, I didn't see why Mother Innana wanted to keep me from what I loved doing. To help me understand it, she had come up with the idea of internships in the city. It had allowed me to meet the man of my life, but not to make me want to become Matriarch. That day, I felt carried by the inhabitants of Dawo, by Theodossis, by Furumark, by Isthar and even by the Mycenaeans. I was ready because I knew what I could give them.

"You don't say anything. Do you want to think about it?"

"It is useless, Mother. It is with great pride that I accept the honour they are giving me."

"I had no doubts ... even though your silence scared me a little. All you have to do now is announce your decision and the name of Matriarch you have chosen... and celebrate with them. Mother Innana would be happy to see what you have accomplished. She was not wrong. Like her, I am sure that you will be a good Matriarch. And who knows? Maybe you will succeed me. That would allow you to reunite Payto and Dawo."

I was about to protest, she cut me off.

"We are not there yet. There is something more pressing that concerns me. Kunisuu and Opsjia are still under Mycenaean administration. In Kunisuu, Iorgos does not evacuate his troops and he already behaves as the governor of the city. I suspect he wants to settle in Kephti."

"He won't be able to stay. Furumark confirmed to me that he would have him return to Mycenae. He even told me that he intended to revoke him."

"We cannot take the risk. To restore the Great Federation, we must re-establish the matriarchies of all the cities, and help the Matriarchs of Chaminjia and Dikta to revive their cities."

"You can count on me, Mother, and I know we can count on Furumark too."

"We will meet again later to begin our actions. Let us first celebrate the liberation of Kephti and the birth of the city of Dawo."

§

Sin-Andul gathered everyone in the Central Square to officially announce the news. The words "our city" triggered an explosion of joy. They shouted, cried, sang. Then they began to chant my name. With great gestures Sin-Andul made them understand that he wanted to speak again.

"I share your enthusiasm for the birth of our new city and for the designation of our Matriarch. But we can no longer call her by the name you chant. Asiraa must now tell us the name of Matriarch she has chosen so that we can express our confidence for her in the forms of our tradition."

I had spent the whole night searching for a name and preparing my speech. I couldn't remember anything. The intensity of their waiting was paralyzing me. My first words choked in my throat. Across from me, holding Melina in his arms, Theodossis was looking at me encouragingly. He came over to me and whispered:

"Melina wants to tell you something."

He brought her close to my ear. She whispered, "You're beautiful, Mom." Tears welled up in my eyes. I knew they could see it. I took advantage of that to launch myself.

"As you can see, I am very moved. Because of Melina, … and especially because of you who are giving me the greatest honor for a Hattiantean. Queen Nanaya had fled her country ravaged by war to come to Hattiarina and found her new city. We fled from the furies of nature and, like her, we are going to found our city. In memory of those times that those of today echo, I have chosen to take the name of the first Matriarch of Urukinea. Her name was Issasara."

Immediately, they declaimed in unison the traditional welcome of the new Matriarch:

"Long life, wisdom and clairvoyance to Mother Issasara."

Then I had just enough time to tell them that I had asked Sin-Andul to be my General Intendant. I thought I would continue by warning them about the heavy reconstruction tasks that remained to be carried out and, above all, about the difficulties to be feared regarding the relations between the Hattianteans and the Mycenaeans, but the jubilation had already set the Central Square on fire. For three days and three nights, Payto and Dawo celebrated together the liberation of Kephti and the birth of our city.

§

With Mother Ninkilim, we decided to call a conference bringing together the active Matriarchs and the Mycenaean general staff in Kephti. Since Furumark was still in Mycenae, our interlocutor could only be Iorgos. We had the greatest difficulty in meeting him. Either our messengers were turned away under the pretext that the rawateka was travelling in another city, or they were given an evasive answer, promising that he would make himself available soon. By dint of insistence, he finally gave in. The conference was held in Gortunjia. After making us wait for a good hour, Iorgos entered, without apologizing for his delay and making us understand that we were disturbing him. I was supposed to speak first but I was so exasperated that, in order not to risk provoking an incident, I preferred to let Mother Ninkilim speak. More diplomatic than I, she began by expressing the gratitude of the Hattiantean people towards the Mycenaean army, then she addressed the thanks of the Matriarchs to the king and his rawateka for their personal involvement in the victory over tyranny. Without transition, she firmly continued on the question of the establishment of the Matriarchs of Opsjia and Kunisuu.

From then on, there was no way to get anything clear. As soon as it was a question of setting dates, Iorgos launched into a long speech on the difficulties of managing an army scattered throughout Kephti, on the insecurity that persisted because of supposed fugitives from Issessinak's troops or on the need to wait for Furumark's return. He always had explanations to justify the impossibility of engaging. In the midst of this flood of evasions and lies, he never missed an opportunity to repeat, with unrestrained bad faith, that all the commitments made by Furumark would be respected.

This unbearable conference made me understand that, starting from our embassy to Mycenae, Iorgos had understood the opportunity that a landing at Kephti could offer him. His evasive attitude was not only a trait of his character, it was the implementation of a long-calculated plan to settle on the island. Now he ignored us and behaved like the governor of Kephti. I did not understand how Furumark could leave us alone to face this sly general whom he himself said he wanted to get rid of. I felt betrayed. He had dangled grandiose plans before me and, as soon as he returned to Mycenae, he had moved on to something else.

Having learned that Iorgos was in Opsjia, I went there alone with the firm intention of explaining myself to him one-on-one. When I arrived, I was shocked to see many armed militiamen in the streets. However, when I questioned passers-by, no one complained about their presence. Some even said they were reassured and, regarding the absence of Matriarch in their city, they were content to assume that it would be temporary. Obviously, Mother Lu-Namhani had left them with such bad memories that they were in no hurry to replace her. Three years of fighting and destruction had exhausted everyone. They could work again, raise their children and party with their friends. The streets were lively, with all their stalls open and well-stocked. It was something they had feared they would never see again. They wanted above all to enjoy it. I was wandering around like this, lost in my questions about this passivity when I found myself surrounded by three militiamen ordering me to follow them. An hour later, I was in front of the rawateka.

"You could have announced yourself when you arrived in my city. A Matriarch who enters on the sly, admits that it is rather curious. And not very diplomatic."

"I didn't know Opsjia was your city. I also see that you are still ignorant of the Hattiantean customs. Let me remind you that in our country, everyone moves freely, whenever they want and wherever they want."

As usual, he spun off long-winded justifications that he himself did not believe. When I asked him about the Opsjia matriarchy, he again mentioned supposed troubles caused by Issessinak's partisans who had remained in the city. He assured me that, when the time came, he would call on me to choose the new Matriarch. Seeking to destabilise him, I offered him an interview with him and the king when he returned.

"Furumark will not return."

"I don't believe you. He swore to me that he would come back."

"The king is dead."

It was like he had punched me in the face. I could only try to hold back my tears to hide my emotion from him. He made the effort to give me some details.

"It happened shortly after his return to Mycenae. He was working with his architects. At the end of the meeting, as he was getting up to leave the table, he was seized with chest pains and collapsed. He died during the night."

§

A few months later, on the occasion of a visit to Mother Nanshe, I saw that Kamaljia had also improved a lot. The refugee camps had shrunk and the grand buildings had regained their splendour. The baths had even been rebuilt. The Matriarch explained to me that Iorgos had helped her a lot. He had sent dozens of soldiers and hundreds of slaves to restore the damaged buildings, rebuild the harbour, and repair the boats. In the countryside, he had the ashes cleared so that the peasants could return to their lands. Of course, she was pleased. When I pointed out to her that he still had not restored the matriarchies of Kunisuu and Opsjia, she rolled her eyes.
"What do you want to do about it? The people are not unhappy. There are no more supply problems and the shops are working more than before thanks to the Mycenaean garrisons. In Dawrometo, the construction of the Mycenaean trading post is well advanced. Ships from Mycenae are already arriving with goods."
In fact, in Mycenae and in all the lands of Argos, the commercial opening of Kephti and the access to Egypt were soon known. Traders flocked and all the cities benefited from this renewed activity. Finally, it looked like what Furumark and I had planned, and I thought that we would perhaps

experience a thousand years of peace and prosperity again. Unfortunately, as I write these lines, thirty years later, I am afraid that this is not the case. What we feared when we considered calling on the army of Mycenae has happened. In Opsjia and Kunisuu, entire districts have become exclusively Mycenaean. In Dawrometo, the trading post that Furumark had planned is like the citadel of Mycenae: an austere and closed fortress, inhabited only by Achaeans. Iorgos has taken all the ports of Kephti under his control and imposes fees on foreigners who come to trade on the island. He has amassed immense wealth and, by placing administrators at his command in the cities, he has dispossessed the Hattianteans of their destiny.

In Kunisuu, he has appropriated the Central House to make it a palace larger and more richly decorated than that of Mycenae. There is nothing left of the Hattiantean spirit in this colourful and pretentious building. This wealth displayed without restraint arouses resentment and jealousy but Iorgos does not care. When people protest, he sends his militia to put an end to the disturbance. He continues to corrupt Achaeans and Hattianteans to extend his influence, without worrying about the tensions that accumulate. His succession already arouses fierce rivalries in his entourage. Defeated by age or by those who covet his power, he will soon no longer be there to dominate the pack. I fear that Kephti will then experience great misfortunes again.

What happened to us? The ravages of the Hattiarina explosion allowed Issessinak to attack the Hattiantean people, then

Iorgos to settle on our lands. Bad luck seems to have befallen us. Yet before the explosion, weren't Opsjia and Kunisuu already ruled by Matriarchs with corrupt minds? Wasn't Issessinak already trying to bring Kunisuu under his thumb? The history of peoples is as much that of the unpredictable moods of nature as that of the whims of their rulers. The Hattiarina explosion, the actions of each of the Matriarchs, my meeting with Furumark, the tyrannical madness of Issessinak, the thirst for wealth and power of Iorgos, have shaped the destiny of the Hattiantean and Mycenaean peoples. Furumak and I had dreamed of extending and prolonging what Queen Nanaya had founded. Perhaps it was no longer possible. The Hattiantean people would never again know the harmony they had experienced for a thousand years, because time changes things and beings, imperceptibly but relentlessly.

The same is true of everyone's destiny. What I have accomplished, I owe to the trust of Mother Inanna, to the chance of having been spared, to the exemplary nature of Mother Nanshe, to the courage of Nin-Gula, to the dreams and affection of Furumark, to the memory of Ninissina, to the loyalty of Sin-Andul and, above all, to the strength, constancy and love of Theodossis. For nothing in the world would I have wanted a life other than the one I lived with him. Fate took almost all my family and all my friends from me. It made up for it by allowing me to love, every day, every hour, even with every beat of my heart, the man I wanted by my side.

In my turn, I will soon be defeated by the illness that took away Isthar, my beloved cousin, my twin. As I approach my departure for the Great City, I remember the little girl who painted frescoes and who preferred to live her romantic impulses rather than face the destiny that Mother Inanna announced to her. She escaped the explosion of Hattiarina. But she did not survive the catastrophe. She was not prepared to face the evil as it appeared to her. She was unaware of its existence. So, in order not to disappear completely, she agreed to become a woman of war then Mother Issasara, Matriarch.

At the end of my life, I still don't believe there is any god to welcome me or judge me in the Great City. I am only certain that I will find there the souls of all those I loved and who were taken from me in one day.

§

EPILOGUE

At the end of the enthusiastic applause generated by Yves Duguy's presentation, Aristotle Kondopoulos takes the floor again.

"Thank you, thank you! I am glad that you appreciate Yves' remarkable work so much. I think that we have not yet finished discovering its consequences. To conclude this congress, I would like to return to the message that Mother Issasara, feeling her end approaching, wished to leave to the inhabitants of Crete."

"She was 17 years old when Santorini erupted. According to the information she gives in her memoirs, we can estimate that she must have been around fifty years old when she died. If we accept the date of 1628 BC for the catastrophe, this means that she died around 1594 BC. She therefore did not experience the destruction that is found in most Cretan cities and that is generally dated to the second half of the 15th century BC, a few decades after her death. However, she describes a situation that allows us to imagine what could have happened."

"Tensions between the two communities, stirred up by clan conflicts after the death of the dictator Iorgos, may have degenerated into a civil war. Knossos (Kunisuu) was the residence of the Mycenaean dictator. The fact that it was relatively spared seems to indicate that it remained the victorious centre of this conflict, thus putting Crete in the hands of the Mycenaeans alone for the following centuries."

"We are coming to the end of this congress. To conclude, I would like to give the floor to the one who saved the memory of her people. Listen to what Mother Issasara has wished to say to the inhabitants of Crete, a little over 3,600 years ago."

True to his sense of showmanship, Aristotle had an actress make an audio recording of Issasara's will. With a sign towards the control room, he starts the broadcast. A woman's voice echoes throughout the room. Those who had started to chat suddenly fall silent. Aristotle himself is visibly surprised by the emotion aroused in him by the very present voice of Mother Issasara.

"I, Issasara, daughter of Eanatum and Nin-Dadda, born Asiraa in the forever vanished city of Urukinea, Matriarch of the city of Payto, on the eve of my departure for the Great City, I hereby address my last wishes to the people of Kephti.

At the dawn of the second millennium of its existence, the Hattiantean people were struck by almost insurmountable natural calamities. The perfidious Intendant Issessinak sought to take advantage of this to enslave them to his tyranny. I then asked for help from King Furumark, prince of the city of Mycenae. Thanks to him, the filthy traitor was defeated and his carcass was thrown onto the mountain so that the vultures could carry the smallest shred of his flesh to hell.

Today, aroused by the greed of the rawateka Iorgos, the rancour and jealousies between the Achaean and Hattiantean peoples grow every day, once again foreshadowing the worst. Do not be caught in the nets of hatred. Like all things, Iorgos and his greedy spirit will disappear. Do not be jealous of his riches and of those of his servants. For their final journey, they will have to leave them on the banks of the Hubur River. Take full advantage of what our land offers you every day and be satisfied with it. The only wealth you can take to the Great City is the love you have received in return for the love you have given.

Let this will be distributed to Kephti in every home, Hattiantean or Achaean. I have it engraved in both our languages, so that everyone can find in it the words that will allow the two peoples to live in peace."

THE END

MIXTE
Papier issu de sources responsables
Paper from responsible sources
FSC® C105338